D0966921

DECADENT DECEIT

DeAnna Julie Dodson

Annie's®

AnniesFiction.com

Decadent Deceit
Copyright © 2015, 2019 Annie's.

All rights reserved. No part of this publication may be reproduced, stored in a retrieval system, or transmitted in any form or by any means—electronic, mechanical, photocopying, recording or otherwise—without the prior written permission of the publisher. The only exception is brief quotations in printed reviews. For information address Annie's, 306 East Parr Road, Berne, Indiana 46711-1138.

The characters and events in this book are fictional, and any resemblance to actual persons or events is coincidental.

Library of Congress-in-Publication Data
Decadent Deceit / by DeAnna Julie Dodson
p. cm.
I. Title
2015908760

AnniesFiction.com
(800) 282-6643
Secrets of the Quilt™
Series Creator: Shari Lohner
Series Editors: Shari Lohner, Janice Tate, and Ken Tate
Cover Illustrator: Jonathan Bouw

10 11 12 13 14 | Printed in China | 9 8 7 6 5

PROLOGUE

Cabot Falls, Vermont
Present Day

> *"Due. Cerise Bélanger, Reggia di Versailles,*
> *Versailles, Francia."*

Sofia Parker looked up from the red leather diary cradled in her hands, the twinkling lights from the Christmas tree adding to the glow in her hazel eyes. The little book, written in Italian over a hundred years ago, was filled with stories from her family's past. And for each story, there was a piece of fabric with a history. Those bits of cloth had been sewn together and made into a quilt. The quilt and the diary had been passed down to Sofia from Nonna, her grandmother, only a short time ago. Nonna had trusted Sofia to care for them, to preserve not only the delicate fabrics but the threads of family history that would otherwise be lost.

Sofia was careful not to hold the book too tightly, knowing it wouldn't take much to damage the timeworn binding and fragile pages, but she couldn't keep her excitement from showing on her face.

Reggia di Versailles. Could it be?

Julie Butler tapped one perfectly manicured fingernail on the rim of her wine glass, her reddish eyebrows raised. "You know neither of us has a clue what that means."

Beside her, Marla Dixon nodded. "Mind translating? I didn't understand a word."

Sofia couldn't help sharing this latest story with her two friends, even though they were officially there to paint. The three of them, though they did call themselves the Pinot Painters, typically did more talking than painting anyway.

"Sorry. It's the story about the second square in the quilt."

She checked the hand-drawn diagram on the diary's first page. Above the top left corner of the central square, marked with a faded number one, was another square, smaller and a little longer than it was wide. This square was number two.

"Reggia di Versailles," she added, "means 'the Palace of Versailles.'"

Marla's blue eyes widened. "Do you think this one has to do with French royalty?"

"Ooh," Julie said. "I hope so."

"We won't know until we read it." Sofia set the book aside, knelt before the *cassone*—the intricately carved Italian wedding trunk that housed both the diary and the quilt—and lifted the lid. "I think we can see this square without taking out the quilt."

Careful to touch only the muslin that protected it, Sofia turned back one corner of the quilt. The three women scarcely breathed as the twinkling light fell on the carefully preserved fabrics pieced together there. Soft greens, shimmering blues, fiery reds and yellows, deep blacks, and rich browns were all dimmed with time but still vibrant. Sofia always marveled at the age of these pieces, some of them reported to be over five hundred years old. And many of them had a connection to someone famous. What was square number two's connection to the Palace of Versailles?

"This one, I think." Sofia pointed to a square of silver silk embroidered with a multitude of golden fleurs-de-lis. "It has to be."

Julie leaned closer and squinted the slightest bit. "How in the world did they get those stitches so tiny?"

"I think that thread is actually made of gold," Marla breathed. "That piece of fabric sure didn't come from an old dishrag."

With a laugh, Sofia settled the quilt back into place and closed the trunk. "Well, I haven't read the story yet, but I do have my suspicions about who this Cerise Bélanger might be."

"Don't tell us you're related to French royalty," Julie said, her emerald eyes twinkling.

Sofia settled into her green- and ivory-striped armchair and picked up the diary again. "Not royalty. Not that I know of. But all my life, I've heard that somewhere in our family tree there was a French countess who lost everything in the revolution and ended up as a penniless refugee in England. I never heard anything else about her, not even her name, but I can't help wondering if this might be her story."

"If she was at Versailles during the French Revolution," Marla mused, "do you think that piece of fabric might have come from one of Marie Antoinette's gowns? That would be amazing."

Julie nodded. "She must have known the queen at least, living at the palace and everything. So, what does it say about her?"

Sofia opened the little book once more and turned the yellowed pages until she was back at the beginning of the second story.

"*Due. Cerise Bélanger, Reggia di Versailles, Versailles, Francia.*"

She struggled with some of the words, but she was sure she was getting most of it right. Cerise was the daughter of Jean-Paul Bélanger, Vicomte Proulx, sent to the court of King Louis XVI and Queen Marie Antoinette to find herself a husband.

Julie chuckled. "I guess it's always good to have a plan," she said. "What does 'due' mean?"

"It means to owe, or to have a debt, I think," Sofia said.

"According to this, Cerise was an only child. Being female, she couldn't inherit her father's title and property."

"It would have all gone to her father's closest male relative." Marla frowned, thinking. "If I remember correctly."

"Exactly," Julie said. "So, off she goes to try to marry well."

"But she must have, if she ended up being a countess, as I've always heard," Sofia said. "I suppose—"

The mantel clock began to strike, and Julie glanced at her watch. "I'd love to hear more, but I have to get going. I have an early meeting in the morning."

"I had no idea it was so late," Marla said. "I'd better get a good night's sleep so I don't look too scary for my blind date."

Julie grinned at her. "Oh, the dreaded blind date."

"I'm not sure I'm ready for this," Marla admitted with a sigh. "I mean, at my age . . ."

"At your age?" Sofia chuckled. "You're forty-eight! You make it sound like you're pushing a hundred. You go and enjoy yourself. It's way past time, and Ryan would have told you the same thing."

Marla nodded, looking down, and then she gave Sofia a wry smile. "You're right. He would have." She ate the last bite of Sofia's homemade tiramisu on her plate. "Anyway, it was delicious as always, Sofia. And you'll have to let us know what else you find out about your countess. If I know you, you'll stay up all night trying to translate."

Sofia stood up. "Not tonight, I'm afraid. I have an early meeting too."

Marla and Julie also stood.

"Is it about the play?" Marla asked as she gathered plates and glasses. "I didn't think that meeting was until next week."

"No," Sofia said. "Next week, both of my sisters and their families are coming to town for Christmas." She and Julie joined Marla in cleaning up. "Tomorrow I'm meeting with the director of the play, a mother of one of the students. I've already met with the teacher about how she wants the sets to look and what needs to be done when."

Soon the room was tidy. It didn't take long since Marla and Julie hadn't even unpacked their painting supplies.

"Sorry we didn't actually get to paint," Sofia said.

Julie laughed. "You'll have plenty of painting to do once you get to work on those sets."

"Let us know if we can help," Marla added. "And let us know what else you find out about your countess."

"Yeah," Julie chimed in. "I always wondered what kind of cake Marie Antoinette let them eat."

"Marie Antoinette didn't actually say that," Marla said.

"What?" Julie was incredulous. "She didn't say, 'Let them eat cake'?"

"It's from Rousseau's *Confessions*, which wasn't actually very reliable. It didn't even name Marie Antoinette."

As Sofia let them out into the frosty night, she heard Julie say to Marla, "I could really go for some cake now."

"Next week," Sofia called out to her. "I'll make one for you."

"Then let *us* eat cake!" Julie exclaimed. "Or cookies. Cookies are good too."

1

Palace of Versailles, France
May 1789

Cerise Bélanger leaned forward as the carriage turned onto Grand Avenue and the Palace of Versailles appeared before her. Even the tales she had heard had not prepared her for the splendor of it, for the endless vista of gardens and lawns, for myriad fountains filled with bronze nymphs and demigods and heroes; for the crowds of people, noble and common alike, going in and out; for the palace itself that shone golden in the spring sunshine and seemed to stretch into eternity.

She opened her mouth, but no sound would come from it. It was all too wonderful. Too amazing. Too terrifying.

"Unless you wish the court to think your father is a fish and not a vicomte, ma chérie, you should close your mouth."

Cerise snapped her mouth shut and then clutched her maid's hand. "Oh, Thérèse, it is . . . I do not even know how to say what it is. I cannot possibly go in."

"Of course you can. Thousands of people do it every day."

"But to attend the queen herself—"

Thérèse sniffed. "You have not been asked to attend the queen, chérie. Only to meet her."

"But Madame la Duchesse—"

"Madame la Duchesse can do nothing but introduce you. Anything more is entirely up to Her Majesty. If she likes you, no doubt you will be invited to stay. And if not?" Thérèse threw up her hands in resignation.

"But she must!" Cerise took hold of her maid's hand once more. "She *must* let me stay. Papa—"

"Shh. We are here."

Thérèse put Cerise's hands in her lap and pushed her back against the cushioned seat as the coach rolled to a stop in front of the entrance. A servant in the king's livery hurried to open the door and handed her out. In the time it took Thérèse to bustle out after her, Cerise found herself set upon by a middle-aged vision in pink taffeta and a beribboned powdered wig.

"Oh, my little Cerise! Is it you, bonbon? Is it you?" The woman seized Cerise's hands and held her arms wide, looking her up and down. "You have outdone your lovely mother, chérie, and that is saying much, though your eyes are the same lovely shade of aquamarine as hers. I daresay the queen will be very pleased."

Yes, this was the Duchesse de Bois d'Archambault, Maman's friend, the one to whom Papa had written about Cerise coming to Versailles, the one who would introduce her to the queen and somehow arrange for her to be invited to stay.

Cerise made a deep curtsy. "Madame la Duchesse, how good of you to come yourself. Everything here is so enormous, I was not certain I would ever be able to find you."

The older woman laughed. "Everyone can find me, bonbon. You need only ask. Now, have you brought it with you?"

Cerise nodded at Thérèse, who patted the bundle of fabric she carried.

"Excellent," the duchesse said. "Now come along. You must refresh yourself in my quarters. Then we shall see if Her Majesty will favor you with an audience."

She hurried Cerise and her maid inside, chattering about the people Cerise simply *must* meet and whom she must avoid. Nobles and commoners alike filled the halls, there to gaze upon royal splendor or in hopes of receiving royal favor. Cerise was careful to stay close to the duchesse, knowing she could never find her way through such a throng if they were separated.

"Are there always so many people?" she asked. She covered her mouth and nose with one hand. "And does it always smell so?"

The duchesse merely shrugged. "They allow anyone in, bonbon, even those who do not bathe. Best to hurry along."

As they passed through the halls of splendor, the duchesse exchanged brief greetings and made introductions with numerous courtiers, many of whom approached her to beg her to take a request to the queen.

"Everyone wants something," she told Cerise. "It is the way of Versailles. You may as well learn that at once."

Cerise dropped her eyes, knowing she had come to ask for favors as well.

The duchesse laughed. "I do not mind, bonbon. For your dear maman, I will do my best for you. But you must remember that before the queen, we are all beggars."

They hurried on until they reached the duchesse's own lovely rooms, not far from the queen's, and Cerise was at last allowed to sit down.

"Now that we are alone," said the duchesse, sitting beside her, "tell me truly why you have come. Your papa, he says only that it is too important to put into a letter."

Cerise glanced at Thérèse, who busied herself with brushing off Cerise's shoes and would not meet her eye.

"As you know, madame," Cerise began, feeling the color come into her face, "when Papa goes on to le bon Dieu, his lands and title will pass to the great-grandson of his grandfather's brother. That is Monsieur Romain Lévesque, Vicomte de Guérin. He is . . . unattached. And, well, perhaps . . ."

The duchesse laughed softly. "Ah, I see." She paused a moment. "Have your maid make you as perfect as possible. I will see if the queen is at her leisure." She smiled at Cerise and hurried out.

"It is a madhouse!" Thérèse exclaimed. "And the king and queen allow it?"

"Surely not all of the palace is the same," Cerise said. "I cannot imagine the common people are allowed in the finer quarters. Oh, how do they bear it? Children running wild everywhere? Dogs too?"

"Never mind the dogs," Thérèse said, tight-lipped. "I saw one rogue using the corridor as if it were a chamber pot!"

"The corridor?" Cerise's eyes widened and she put one hand over her mouth. "Their Majesties must have private apartments and salons where they receive guests away from such things."

"I am sure it is so, chérie." Thérèse brushed dust off her mistress's daffodil-yellow brocade gown. "Still, I would not have expected such bedlam in the palace itself."

Cerise squeezed her eyes shut and turned her face away from the cloud of travel dust Thérèse was stirring up. "I thought we would see more. The grand salons and the chapel."

"In time. In time." Satisfied with the gown, Thérèse helped herself to the pitcher and basin on the duchesse's dressing table and washed Cerise's face and hands. "For now, we must see if we shall be here long enough to take supper."

Cerise looked at her, stricken. "But we *must*. The queen simply must allow me to stay."

"She is the queen, chérie. She has no musts."

Cerise exhaled heavily, frowning as Thérèse's deft hands smoothed her powdered hair, making sure none of the pale blond strands showed through. As a favor to Papa, the duchesse had agreed to bring Cerise to the queen's notice, to perhaps find Cerise a place among Her Majesty's ladies-in-waiting. But Cerise knew those places were much sought after and almost always given only to those of the highest rank and favor. She glanced at the little bundle Thérèse had laid on a side table, and her frown turned into a tiny, hopeful smile. Of course she would never be so favored as to be allowed to actually dress the queen, but perhaps there was a chance her talents would make a place for her after all.

Thérèse had hardly finished reapplying Cerise's face powder and rouge when the duchesse bustled back into the room.

"We are in luck, bonbon. I had feared the queen might be at her little getaway on another part of the grounds, the Petit Trianon, but she is not. She is at this very moment in her salon, and she says she would be delighted to meet you. Now, come at once. Be very quick. She has many important matters to attend to."

Thérèse curtsied to the duchesse and handed Cerise the little bundle of fabric she had carried in the coach. Then, with an almost unnoticeable smile of encouragement, she opened the chamber door.

The duchesse took Cerise's arm and hurried her out into the corridor, chattering all the while, telling her whose quarters they passed, how each person served the queen, who was allowed to hand Her Majesty her chemise, who would put on her jewelry, and so on.

"It is a positive scandal," the duchesse said, her voice dropping to a whisper, "but once the queen has her hair styled, she is dressed by Mademoiselle Bertin, who has no rank whatsoever. But she does have the loveliest taste in clothing. Still"—she clicked her tongue—"it is a disgrace."

In the antechamber, besides the busy servants, there were a number of aristocrats waiting for an audience with the queen, most of them looking with curiosity and even suspicion at the newcomer who dared appear among them. The duchesse paid them no mind as she and Cerise passed through them. Cerise, too, paid little heed to them. Her thoughts were focused on her imminent introduction to the queen herself—until she found her attention drawn to one who seemed unlike the others.

At the end of the room, a young man slouched against the wall. He was nicely dressed, though somewhat more plainly than any of the nobility she had seen up until now. Perhaps he had only recently arrived from the country as she had. Or maybe he was the younger son of one of the lesser nobles, a vicomte with only a small fortune, and had come to court to marry well.

If that was his objective, she was certain he would be successful. He had a handsome face with a square jaw, straight nose, and intelligent eyes that were dark and warm. His hair, too, was dark, pulled back into a neat queue and not powdered. He must have come in from the country.

He straightened when he saw them, and Cerise realized he was taller than she had at first thought, as tall as Papa, but lithe and lean. Certainly he would be successful if he was here to find a bride.

He made a deep bow as they came near. "Madame la Duchesse. Mademoiselle."

When the duchesse made him no acknowledgment, Cerise thought he must be a very minor noble indeed. Still, Cerise gave him a brief nod as they passed him by. It was comforting to think she was not the only one out of place in this glittering palace. It took her a moment to realize that the duchesse was speaking to her.

"Oh, yes, madame." Cerise smiled, scurrying to keep up. "My father has mentioned you very often. He speaks most fondly of you and says he would not dare to send me to court alone if he did not know you were here to look after me."

The duchesse nodded. "Of course, chérie. I knew your papa and dear maman very well during the time of the old king, His Majesty's grand-père. I cannot say I was surprised by your papa's letter last month asking me to see you were taken care of. Given your situation, I thought it would come." They stopped at a closed door and the duchesse turned to Cerise. She put one plump finger under Cerise's chin and turned her face up to the light. "Ah, you do have Annette's pretty looks, I see. The queen will be pleased. Always she must have beauty about her. As long as you are stylish and discreet and do as you are told, you should get along very well here." The older woman put her finger to her rouged lips, considering, and then she smiled. "Now, wait here a moment. I will see if Her Majesty is ready to receive you."

She gave the door a pert knock and was admitted at once, the door closing behind her as quickly as it had opened. *What will she be like, this queen?*

Cerise knew the story, of course, of the youngest daughter of Maria Theresa, the Austrian empress, and Francis I, the Holy Roman Emperor. A girl of fourteen, Maria Antonia Josepha Johanna, as the queen had been christened, had been sent to France to marry the Dauphin, Louis-Auguste, and ensure peaceful relations between the two countries. Rechristened Marie Antoinette, the new Dauphine had enchanted all of France with her youth, her beauty, and her blend of charm, grace, and spirit.

But that had been nineteen years ago, the year before Cerise was born. All Cerise knew of the queen now was what she heard whispered among the servants and in the streets—that the queen was vain and frivolous, emptying the national treasury for her whims, indifferent to the sufferings of her people, engaging in every sort of immorality with her favorites. It seemed that every day the scandal sheets, the *libelles*, grew more outrageous in their accusations. Thérèse, of course, would never let Cerise see such unseemly publications, but Cerise knew there was talk. There was always talk. But what would she find behind that door when at last she met the Queen of France?

Cerise sighed. Was there nothing to do at court but wait?

"You came to be a lady-in-waiting, did you not, mademoiselle?"

Startled, she turned to see the young man from earlier looking at her. He was not quite smiling, but there was humor in his dark eyes. Had he read her thoughts?

"Monsieur?"

"All who serve wait, mademoiselle. High and low, are we not all the humble servants of our king and queen?"

She felt a little warmth creep into her cheeks, but she bowed her head. "Indeed, monsieur. You are . . . you are waiting for an audience?"

One corner of his mouth twitched. "Truly, mademoiselle—"

"Cerise!" The duchesse's smile faded when she saw Cerise was speaking to the man she had snubbed. "You mustn't keep Her Majesty waiting, chérie. Monsieur, you are insolent."

"I beg your pardon, madame," the man said, bowing, and he moved a few feet farther away from the door.

"Now," said the duchesse, smiling again, "let me look at you once more." She rearranged the lace at Cerise's neckline and then gathered up her powdered curls and let them fall artlessly, but not too artlessly, over one shoulder. "Now bite your lips and pinch your cheeks and come along. Remember to smile."

She tugged Cerise's arm, accidentally making her pinch one cheek a little harder than the other. Cerise was certain she had enough color in her face as it was, but there was nothing to do but hurry through the doors and into the presence of the queen.

2

Palace of Versailles, France
May 1789

The Salon des Nobles was crowded with ladies, their wide skirts jostling as they subtly tried to outshine one another and catch the attention of the queen. In the midst of them sat the queen herself, radiant in white silk and diamonds, her hair powdered but not in the fantastic three-foot pouf Cerise had expected.

Having always heard of her remarkable grace, Cerise was surprised to see the queen was tall. Though tending toward stoutness, she had an exquisite figure and the loveliest ivory skin Cerise had ever seen. Her eyes were blue, and there was rather more a sadness in them than the merriment Cerise had expected. But then she remembered the illness of the queen's son, the little Dauphin, and felt a twinge of sympathy for her. There seemed to be nothing about her to indicate she was as wild and licentious as the libelles claimed.

Cerise made her deepest curtsy.

"My queen," the duchesse said, "may I present to you Cerise Bélanger, daughter of Jean-Paul Bélanger, Vicomte Proulx."

"You are welcome to Versailles, Mademoiselle Bélanger." The queen smiled, displaying even, white teeth. "Madame la Duchesse tells me you wish to serve here at court."

Cerise bowed her head. "If it pleases you, Your Majesty, I would like that very much."

The queen turned her smile on a young man who stood to her left. "I see you would like that as well, Gaspard."

Like the man Cerise had spoken to outside in the corridor, this one was tall and lithe, dark-eyed and smooth-featured, but there the resemblance ended. From his powdered wig and lace cravat to his diamond-buckled, high-heeled shoes and walking cane with its tasseled cord, this one was everything Cerise had expected in a gentleman of the court. He studied Cerise with unabashed interest.

"Indeed, my queen. Your own loveliness shines the brighter when surrounded by beauty."

"Mademoiselle," the queen told Cerise with a hint of an arch smile, "you must meet my chief flatterer, Gaspard Valérian, Comte de Therin-Toussant."

The comte immediately seized Cerise's hand and pressed his lips to it. "Enchanted, mademoiselle."

Again Cerise curtsied. "Monsieur."

He turned to the duchesse, bowing deeply. "Madame, how long has it been? And where did you find this pretty one? Surely le bon Dieu is missing one of his angels."

Cerise's lashes swept to her burning cheeks, but the duchesse merely laughed.

"Ah, Gaspard, can you believe her mother and I were girls together? And now, what have we here, but the daughter comes to court, a woman grown. How can that be when I am yet so young?"

The comte laughed politely and again looked at Cerise. "You will be an ornament to the court."

"You honor me, Monsieur le Comte," she replied, "but when the court has already Her Majesty to grace it, any other ornamentation is unnecessary."

"I see your manners are as pretty as your face, mademoiselle," the queen observed, chuckling softly. "Now tell me, what is it you do besides look decorative?"

"I play the clavichord, Your Majesty, but very badly."

The queen fluttered her fan dismissively. "Oh, the court is full of musicians, so we need not trouble you, petite. What I must know, though, is if you play faro. I must warn you, my ladies play like fiends."

The comte gave the queen a sly grin. "Perfect cutthroats, my queen. You really ought not throw this innocent lamb into their path."

"No, Your Majesty," Cerise said, glancing at the duchesse, hoping for some kind of guidance. "I think I am not very good at such games."

"Pity," said the queen, the motion of her fan suddenly languid. "Then what is it you do?"

Again Cerise looked at the duchesse, who now gave her an encouraging nod.

"I am told I do very well with my needle, Your Majesty." She took the fine fabric folded over her arm and, with a curtsy, offered it to the queen. "If I may, it is a gift for you."

The queen's smile was more gracious than interested, but her expression changed as she spread the fabric over her brocade skirts. It was merely a petticoat, but Cerise hoped her hours of painstaking work embroidering it with tiny leaves and flowers had made it fit for a queen.

"This is quite lovely," the queen said at last, touching the delicate stitches with one white finger. "And you did it all yourself?"

Cerise ventured the tiniest smile. "Yes, Your Majesty, so please you."

The queen plucked Cerise's sleeve, which was adorned with finely stitched vines and hundreds of tiny clusters of grapes in exquisite whitework over the soft yellow brocade. "Perhaps you did this as well, chérie?"

"Yes, Your Majesty." Cerise ducked her head, not wanting to seem overly proud. "It is my own design."

"Well, well," the queen said, genuine pleasure in her expression now. "There may be more to your little protégé than first meets the eye, Florianne. I see she shall ornament our court in more than one way." She touched the stitches again. "Perhaps she might be persuaded to add a touch of this to more than her own gowns."

"Naturally, my queen." The duchesse beamed as if she herself had taught Cerise to sew. "What you will."

Cerise kept her eyes lowered, not daring to hope. "It would be my very great honor, Your Majesty."

"Very well then." The queen nodded, clearly in dismissal. "You must take care to do as her father asked and watch over her while she is with us."

The comte had been standing by all this while, a simper covering his obvious boredom at the talk of needlework, but now he stepped forward and bowed. "If Your Majesty will allow me, I will add my efforts to those of Madame la Duchesse." He took Cerise's arm, his smile turning sly. "We cannot have such a treasure go unguarded."

The queen raised one eyebrow, blue eyes twinkling. "And yet, should we set the fox to guard the chicks?" She chuckled as he began to protest. "No, no, no. You will do well enough to look after the child, Gaspard. Run away now, all of you. I have things I must attend to."

"Your Majesty." He bowed, still holding her arm.

Cerise made a deep curtsy, and beside her the duchesse did the same.

The servants swung the doors open, and they were once more in the Salon des Nobles.

"You did well, bonbon," the duchesse crowed. "Very well. I told you she would admire your stitching. Soon she will ask you to embellish one of her own gowns, mark my word, and then you will be made."

"Do you think . . ." Cerise's lips trembled. "Do you think she liked me?"

"She admired your cleverness with a needle, chérie."

"And if you are a wise little girl," the comte added, "you will let that admiration ripen into royal favor." He looked her up and down without the slightest pretense of subtlety. "And royal favor is the golden key that unlocks many doors. Who knows what advantages and opportunities it might bring you?"

Her cheeks turned fiery hot, and she looked away from him, noticing instead the young man she had spoken to earlier still waiting near the wall. Now he was standing straight rather than lounging against it. Instead of amusement, she was certain she saw fury in those dark eyes. But his face betrayed absolutely no emotion. He might have been one of the queen's doormen, simply an automaton.

She dropped her eyes to the floor. "Please, monsieur, I would never presume—"

"Oh, indeed you would, ma belle," the comte said, laughing. "Else why would you have come?"

She could think of nothing to say to that, for truly she had come for no other reason.

"Stop badgering the child, Gaspard." The duchesse pulled her away from him, taking Cerise's arm herself. "Give her a moment to catch her breath before you decide her future. Come, chérie."

"I must see to my own preparations, if you will both pardon me." The comte bowed deeply. "Madame." He bowed again, this time with a ghost of a smirk on his lips. "Mademoiselle." Then he nodded to the man waiting there. "Dieudonné."

The other man was immediately at his heels, and both of them disappeared around the turn in the corridor.

"La, chérie, you shock me," the duchesse scolded. "You will not find you improve yourself here by consorting with the wrong people."

Cerise frowned, puzzled. "Wrong? Do you speak of the gentleman who left with the comte? Who is he?"

"Pretty enough, I suppose," the older woman said, pursing her lips, "but that's of no matter. Surely you could tell at once that he is not of the nobility."

"I . . . no, madame, I merely thought he was waiting for an audience with the queen."

"He?" The duchesse laughed. "The comte's valet?"

Cerise put both hands over her mouth, covering a gasp. "Oh, madame! Madame! How could I have been so foolish? I thought . . . he seemed . . ."

"There now, chérie, you mustn't fret. I imagine a nobleman in the country might not dress as well as the servants here at court. And Monsieur le Comte, he is most particular about clothing for himself and his servants. He's the envy of every gentleman in Versailles for his sense of style. I have heard it is this Alexis Dieudonné who makes him so admired."

Despite herself, Cerise was happy to hear this about the valet.

"Do not fret, bonbon," the duchesse continued. "There was no one to see you speaking to him besides ourselves. Still, you must not make that mistake again."

"No. Most certainly I will not."

"There now, don't look so like a newly caught rabbit, chérie." The duchesse took both of Cerise's hands and squeezed them warmly. "Before long, you will know your way about as if you had been all your life at court."

The very next day in her chamber, Cerise received a letter from her father. No doubt he had sent it shortly after her departure from home.

> *Ma chère fille,*
> *I pray that when this letter reaches you it finds you well and happily settled at court. I would not burden you unnecessarily, but it grieves me to say that things here at Sauveterre are not good. We have many times discussed the declining state of my health, but over the past few days it has grown steadily worse. Old Herriot tells me, as he has these past five years, that I cannot live to see another harvest. This time I feel the truth of it in my bones and in my cooling blood. This time I believe him.*
>
> *No, do not think to return home. Matters are not yet so dire as that, but it becomes more and more difficult for me to write my own letters. Even so, I would rest more comfortably knowing you fare well where you are.*
>
> *I have written to Vicomte Romain Lévesque suggesting that now would be a good time to resume our discussion of three years ago, but he has yet to favor me with his reply. I am certain Madame la Duchesse is doing all in her power to present you to the right people, but of course, this takes time. I pray it is time that I yet have left to me. My poor petite, you do not know how it grieves me to lay such a burden on your dainty shoulders, but my own are not equal to the task. I pray you will not fail.*
> *Votre Père*

Cerise let her hand and the letter fall into her lap. "Oh, Papa, must I?"

Yet she knew the answer already. It was for this she had come to Versailles. For Papa and for herself. But the reality of this place and of these people was more intimidating than she had expected. Yet what else could she do? With her father not long to be with her and with no brother or husband to protect her, what else could she do? Even so, she was not yet ready to meet Vicomte Lévesque, not until she did not feel so awkward here at the palace. She could not waste her precious first impression by proving to him she was a graceless country mouse completely unsuited to court life. She needed more time.

She went to her writing desk and took out a fresh sheet of paper. Then she opened her little bottle of ink and dipped a quill into it.

> *Mon chèr Papa,*
> *I know we have spoken of this often, but knowing you feel the time is at last here grieves me more than I can say. Please do not fret yourself over me or over our dear Sauveterre. I am certain Vicomte Lévesque and I will reach an understanding before very long.*

She continued to fill her letter with assurances of her certain success in an attempt to lift his burden and lighten his heart. She hated not telling him the whole truth, but she did not want to disappoint him or worry him unnecessarily. Not now.

As soon as the letter was sealed, she looked around for Thérèse, hoping it could be sent off right away. But her maid had gone to see when the banquet was to begin. Perhaps one of the doormen or a porter would be able to see to the letter instead.

Cerise crept out into the corridor, feeling somehow as if she would be caught and punished for daring to leave her appointed chamber. *Don't be ridiculous*, she told herself. *The queen was pleased with the petticoat. She was gracious and welcoming. What should I fear?*

The passageway was quiet. No doubt most everyone was already making elaborate preparations to dine with the king and queen, preparations that required the aid of many servants.

She smiled faintly as she heard voices from the other side of a door. Perhaps this door led to another corridor where someone could help her. She put her hand to the latch and then froze.

"We cannot forever be silent," a man said, his voice barely loud enough for her to make out the words. "The people will speak, before or after blood is shed."

Someone inside shushed him, and then she heard footsteps coming toward the door. She scrambled around the next corner and then, peering back, she saw Alexis Dieudonné, the comte's valet, come out. He unfastened the little red, white, and blue cockade from his lapel, stuffed it into his waistcoat pocket, and then hurried away.

3

Cabot Falls, Vermont
Present Day

Sofia hadn't known what to expect when she stepped into the auditorium at Luke's school, but it wasn't this. Usually these productions were marked by frantic, barely controlled chaos until opening night. Then, if Providence smiled, somehow they worked well enough to be deemed a success. Today, though, she saw no sign of chaos. Luke and the other children were sitting together in the two front rows of seats as a tall, rather imposing woman only a little older than Sofia spoke to them.

She had to be Kenny's mother, Naomi Moore, the director of the production. Luke hadn't said a lot about her. Evidently, Kenny didn't talk about her much either.

Sofia smiled and waved as she carried her paints down the aisle toward the stage. "Sorry I'm—"

Naomi held up one finger as if Sofia were one of the twelve-year-olds speaking out of turn. "We're not ready to go onstage yet. If you'd like to sit down in one of the front rows, we will get started soon."

Sofia's smile turned awkward. She obediently sat at the end of the second row, hands folded in her lap, as Naomi finished her instructions about how rehearsals were to be conducted and what was expected of each of them.

"I promise I raised my hand before I excused myself," someone whispered in her ear. She turned and smiled at her husband.

"I was wondering where you were," she whispered back as he sat down next to her. "I was afraid you'd been sent to the principal's office."

Jim laughed softly, blue eyes twinkling behind his glasses, and then broke off, seeing Naomi had stopped talking and was looking expectantly at them both. "Sorry."

Naomi gave them a gracious if slightly reproving smile. "All right, Kenny," she said to the boy sitting directly in front of her. "You hand out the scripts, and we'll get started."

Sofia recognized the boy now. He had dark blond hair and blue eyes like his mother and a gangly, awkward frame like so many boys his age. He'd been over to play with Luke a time or two. He was always polite and well behaved, and the two boys had gotten along well.

"You must be Luke's mother," Naomi said after joining them in the auditorium aisle. "I'm Naomi Moore."

"Sofia Parker. This is my husband, Jim. He teaches math at the high school."

"Good to meet you," Jim said, standing up. "Okay if I get started now?"

Naomi's smile tightened slightly. "Certainly. I understand you have all the sets planned out already. I'm sure they'll be lovely. Do you have sketches?"

"Oh, of course." Sofia pulled out her sketchbook from her bag. "It's just the usual—the nursery, the night sky over London, the forest in Neverland, the treehouse, that sort of thing."

She flipped the pages, pointing out various features required by the script, and was pleased to see Naomi's taut smile soften into one of actual appreciation.

"I was told you're a painter. I don't think the title does you justice. You're a real artist."

"Thank you," Sofia said, a little overwhelmed by the unexpected praise. "But Jim's the real artist. Without him, I wouldn't have anything to paint, and our Peter Pan wouldn't be able to fly."

"Luke and I will do our best," Jim said.

"Luke?" Naomi looked down at her clipboard, searching her cast list. "I thought he was supposed to be one of the Lost Boys. No?"

"I don't think so," Sofia said, looking at the list too. "He told me he wanted to help with the sets, and his teacher was fine with that."

Frowning, Naomi flipped the page over. "Oh, there he is, under 'Crew.' All right. Well, we'd better get under way. Parents will be here before we know it."

"Good," Jim said. "If you think anything we're doing won't work for the play, let me know. We'll figure out a way around it."

Now it was Naomi who looked faintly surprised. "Thank you. Actually, it looks great at this point. If we get into rehearsal and find something won't work, we can talk about it then. Sound good?"

Jim nodded, smiling. "That'll work. Is it okay if we get going on it? I'd like to get some basic framework up."

"Certainly," Naomi replied. "Thanks."

"Luke!" Jim motioned toward the stack of plywood and two-by-fours piled at the back of the stage. "Ready to get to work?"

With a grin, Luke hurried to his father's side. "Are we going to rig the thing that makes him fly?"

"Not yet," Jim said, chuckling. "Gotta have something for him to fly in front of first. Come on."

"Well, I suppose I don't have to worry about the sets at least," Naomi said as she watched them climb the steps to the stage.

Then she turned to the kids and clapped her hands. "All right, everyone. Today we're going to start out by reading through the script and talking about the characters we'll be playing and how to bring them to life. If you're in group one, please move to the front row. Group two, I want you in the second row. Quickly, please."

As the kids jostled around, Naomi turned back to Sofia. "I'm looking forward to seeing your work life-size."

"I hope you like it."

"I'm sure I will." Naomi watched Luke and Jim as they consulted the plans Jim had drawn up. "The three of you make a pretty good team."

Sofia nodded. "I think so."

Naomi's expression turned a little wry as she muttered, "Must be nice."

"Luke says Naomi and Kenny's dad are divorced. For a couple of years now." Sofia dumped the spaghetti into the strainer, turning her face from the steam that billowed up from the sink. "Evidently Kenny hasn't heard from his dad in nearly that long."

"That's too bad," Jim replied. "You'd hope the guy could at least show up at Christmas."

He didn't say anything else for a few minutes, but she could tell by the set of his mouth and the way he yanked open the oven door that he wasn't quite through. "Not much of a father to drop out of his kid's life like that." He took the chicken parmigiana out of the oven and set it on the stove top, leaning down to breathe in the aroma. That seemed to lighten his mood a bit. "I guess you never know about other people's lives though. Maybe he has his reasons."

She tasted the meat sauce and then added a pinch of oregano. "I suppose, although I can't imagine any reason being good enough to excuse that behavior. Kenny seemed awfully interested in what you and Luke were building. A lot more interested than he was in being in the play."

"Can't blame him."

She put one hand on her hip, fighting a smile. "And why do you say that? He's got the lead role."

"Yeah, but what self-respecting twelve-year-old boy wants to run around in green tights?"

Sofia laughed. "He must have known about the costume before he auditioned for the role. What else would Peter Pan wear? He still wanted to do it."

"Maybe," Jim said with a grin and a shrug. "Or maybe he liked the idea of flying. He seemed very interested in how we were going to do that."

"He's probably like most boys his age, eager to find out about everything but hard to keep on task." She lifted the lid on the pot where the corn on the cob was boiling to make sure it wasn't overdone, and then she looked toward the living room. "That reminds me. Luke? Matt? Come and set the table, please."

"Aww, Mom!" the boys wailed in chorus.

"Right now, please," she said, going to the door. *"Horrible Zombie-Eating Mutant Dinosaurs from Space* can wait until after dinner and after homework."

Luke and Matthew trudged into the kitchen.

"That's not the name of the game," Matthew said as he opened the silverware drawer.

"Pink Pony Dress-Up Playland?" Jim suggested, reaching over his head to get a stack of plates from the cabinet and then handing them to Luke.

"Very funny, Dad," Luke deadpanned with a roll of his dark eyes.

Jim ruffled his hair. "Want to help me with my flying machine tonight?"

Luke nodded eagerly. "Does that mean we get to test it out?"

"I want to try it!" Matthew bounced up and down on the balls of his feet, silverware still clutched in his hand. "Can I, Dad?"

"You've got homework," Sofia singsonged, turning him back toward the table.

"So does Luke," Matthew whined.

"This *is* for school, bean brain," Luke said, jostling his little brother out of the way so he could set a plate between the knife and fork already on the table.

"Be nice, Luke." Sofia poured the spaghetti into a bowl and then dumped the boiled ears of corn into the empty strainer. "And the play comes *after* your other schoolwork. Yes, you're supposed to help build sets, I know, but homework comes first. Now, do me a favor and get your sisters."

Luke went to the kitchen door and slouched against the frame. "Hey, Vanessa! Time to eat! Get Wynter!"

"Excuse me?" Jim raised one eyebrow at his older son. "Mom asked you to get the girls, not bust everybody's eardrums. *Now.*"

Luke winced. "Yeah. Right. Sorry, Mom."

He shot out of the kitchen, and Sofia shook her head. "He gets that from you, you know."

"Nah," Jim said as he transferred the chicken to a serving platter. "All he gets from me are rakish good looks and devastating charm."

"Don't forget modesty," she added, nudging his ribs with her elbow.

Soon the entire family was gathered at the table.

"You have your therapy appointment tomorrow, Wynter," Sofia told her younger daughter when everyone had full plates. "We'll have to hurry if I'm going to get you there in time to take Matthew to Jeff's before I go to work on the sets for the play. Daddy will have to pick you up afterward."

Wynter nodded her dark head, smiling slightly. Since her cochlear implant surgery, her hearing had improved well beyond the doctors' most optimistic expectations, but she still tended to rely on nods and sign language.

"You know," Vanessa said in her most nonchalant voice, "if I got a car for Christmas, I could drive everybody wherever they needed to go. It would really be more for Mom than for me." She looked at her dad with guileless green eyes.

He grinned at her. "Good try, sweetie, but not till somebody leaves us a small fortune."

She gave him an exaggerated pout and then giggled. "Had to try." She put an ear of corn on her plate. "Did you read any more of your diary, Mom? We've been studying the French Revolution in history, and it sounds pretty scary."

"They didn't call it 'The Terror' for nothing," Jim said as he buttered his bread. "And absolute power corrupts absolutely, whether those in power are the nobility or the revolutionaries."

"I'm going to read some more tonight," Sofia said. "But I guess the girl in the diary must have gotten through it. Otherwise, how could she have ended up as a penniless seamstress in England?"

"Maybe the Scarlet Pimpernel got her out," Luke suggested, eyes bright.

Sofia chuckled. "You know he wasn't real, right?"

Luke frowned and prodded a slice if chicken with his fork. "Well, it would have been more fun if he was."

"If she and Count Whoever-it-was got to England early enough, maybe it wasn't so bad for them," Sofia said.

"But if they had to leave everything behind," Jim said, "then things must have been pretty far gone already, don't you think?"

Sofia smiled. "I suppose I'll have to read more and find out."

4

Palace of Versailles, France
May 1789

The royal banquet had been a great success. Cerise was introduced to a dizzying array of nobility and royalty along with a particular variety of champagne that left her feeling rather queasy the next morning. She did not know if she had been disappointed or relieved when she learned that Vicomte Romain Lévesque had been in Paris that night and she would not have the honor—or the duty—of meeting him. Not yet.

The morning after the banquet was warm and bright. She was happy to sit in the garden, breathe the fresh air, and have a moment of peace. Thérèse sat at her side, mending the hem in one of Cerise's chemises, mercifully silent. Cerise herself sat with a piece of rose-colored silk wadded in her lap. She was meant to be embellishing it with fine silver thread for a robe for the queen, but she found she was picking out at least half of the stitches she put in. Instead, she watched one of the gardener's helpers, a boy of perhaps ten, carry bucket after bucket of water for the flowers that grew nearby.

"Pretty," a man's voice said. She looked up to see the Comte de Therin-Toussant bowing over her, a smile on his handsome face. "Very pretty."

Warmth crept into Cerise's cheeks. "Monsieur?"

"The gardens, mademoiselle. Are they not lovely?"

"Yes, certainly. And do you often walk here, monsieur?"

There was a sudden slyness in his smile. "Only when there is something worth my notice. I had hoped you might do me the honor of walking with me, but I see you are occupied."

She glanced again at the boy with the water. He had stopped to mop the sweat from his brow with his soiled sleeve, but he scurried back to work when he caught Cerise's gaze.

She sighed. "I seem to be having a little trouble coaxing my eyes and my hands into cooperating with each other."

"I see. Perhaps they would be improved if you were to take the air for half an hour, no?"

She hadn't liked the way the comte looked at her at the banquet last night, and she liked it even less now that there was no one but Thérèse nearby. But then again, he was an important man and a favorite of the queen herself. Surely it would be unwise to miss the opportunity to have his patronage and friendship—and even more unwise to make of him an enemy.

She smiled, stood, and put the rose-colored silk into her basket. "That would be most kind of you, monsieur."

He bowed and offered his arm, which she accepted, and they began to walk.

"And how are you enjoying Versailles?"

"It is rather overwhelming. I have never met so many of France's nobles."

One corner of his mouth turned up. "There do seem to be a great many of them. It seems every hostler and innkeeper has a title these days."

She suspected that the great Comte de Therin-Toussant no doubt had little regard for the daughter of a mere vicomte, but perhaps he would be kind nonetheless.

"I . . . I had hoped to meet my cousin Romain, the Vicomte de Guérin, but they tell me he will be in Paris a while longer."

The comte sneered. "Guérin? I did not know you were related."

"It is rather a distant relation, monsieur, though he will come into my father's property once Papa has gone on to his reward."

Her escort laughed softly. "Ah, now I see. And you are to be the sacrificial lamb. Surely, ma belle, you can do better than that cloth-headed popinjay."

"Monsieur!" she objected.

"No, no, ma belle, do accept my apologies. But you have been here a very short while. Perhaps fortune has in mind something far better for you."

"I take it you and my cousin are not friends?"

The comte sneered. "Monsieur le Vicomte is friends with all the world. He drinks and gambles with the Duc d'Orléans as easily as with the villain who gathers the king's firewood, and he insults them both alike. It is all one to him."

Before she could ask him what he meant, his valet, Dieudonné, came toward them with swift, long strides. He bowed deeply, keeping his eyes on the ground.

"I beg your pardon, mademoiselle," Dieudonné said, then addressed the comte. "You wished to be advised when Monsieur Chambertin arrived. He is in the small salon even now, if you are pleased to come."

The comte's dark eyes lit. "Ah, excellent." He turned toward Cerise. "I pray you pardon me, petite, but the matter is urgent."

"I hope there is nothing wrong."

"Oh no. Monsieur Chambertin is my tailor. He is doing the final fitting for my new waistcoat. I absolutely must have it done in time for the grand ball the queen is giving tonight, even if it means our most delightful meeting must end."

He bent to kiss her hand. Stepping back to give her his courtliest bow, he upset the water boy's bucket and doused his own diamond-buckled shoe.

"What have you done!" he demanded with a curse, seizing the boy by the hair and yanking him to his feet. "I shall have the skin flayed from your miserable back!"

The boy shrank back in terror. "Your pardon, monsieur. I . . . I . . ."

Dieudonné put his hand on the boy's thin shoulder, putting himself between the boy and the comte. "Forgive me, monsieur, the fault is mine. The boy's work brought him to this part of the garden. He merely meant to show his respect by kneeling as you passed. I should have warned you he was there behind you."

"Out of my way, Dieudonné!" the comte spat, adding an oath. "I'll teach these dogs respect!"

The boy ducked his head, bracing himself, but the valet did not move.

"If you must strike someone, let it be me." Dieudonné's eyes flicked toward Cerise and then turned again to his master. "But let it be out of the sight of the lady. Surely she has no pleasure in such matters."

There was such a resemblance between the two men, a likeness in height and build and bearing, but otherwise they seemed nothing alike. The valet's face was all calm reason. His master's was pure and unbridled rage. But then, as if he suddenly remembered himself, the comte's face changed.

"A trifle," he said, smiling tightly at Cerise and giving a negligent wave of his hand. "Do not be disturbed."

Dieudonné knelt at his master's feet and blotted the offended shoe with his handkerchief while keeping himself between the boy and the comte. "Do not forget Monsieur Chambertin, monsieur. The new waistcoat ought not be delayed, and we must see you have fresh shoes and stockings first."

The boy dropped to his knees again, looking as if he were trying to make himself as small and unnoticeable as possible, but the comte did not spare him another glance.

"Very true. Well, come then. To Monsieur Chambertin. Mademoiselle, I will leave you to enjoy the morning air."

Once again the comte bowed over Cerise's hand.

"Mademoiselle," Dieudonné said with a bow of his own, and then he and his master hurried away.

"It is all right," Cerise said softly when the water boy did not move.

He looked up at her through the lank hair that fell over his forehead.

"It is all right," she said again. "You may get up now."

He merely blinked at her.

She smiled and held out her hand. "What is your name?"

He swallowed hard. "Pardon me, mademoiselle. I am Michel, if you please."

"Very well, Michel. You have done nothing wrong, I promise you. Now hurry back to your work. And stay out of sight when Monsieur le Comte is near, yes?"

He managed a tiny smile. With several more unsteady bows, he grabbed his bucket and darted into the trees. When he was gone, she looked up to see the comte and his valet had reached the palace door. She did not know which of them had surprised her more during their encounter.

When she made her way back to the bench where she had left Thérèse, she found her maid holding a letter sealed with her father's crest, the crest of Sauveterre.

"It has come but now. A special messenger."

A sudden feeling of dread washed over Cerise. "Let us go back inside. I wish to read this alone."

Thérèse gave her arm a sympathetic squeeze. "Of course."

Once they reached her quarters, Thérèse tactfully busied herself with putting fresh sheets on Cerise's bed. In her sitting room, Cerise took a steadying intake of breath and opened the message. She had expected to see her father's sprawling script. Instead, she saw the cramped handwriting of a professional scribe.

> *Ma chère fille,*
> *The time we have feared has come. Do not let this grieve you, ma fille. Only let it turn you more directly toward the task you have in hand. At the end of my life, I see I have nothing but the name I leave and this home I love as if it, too, were a child of mine. I cannot see it lost to you and to the children you will one day bear.*
> *Those children, I know, will never be seen with my natural eyes, but if I know they will walk these halls and these lands, if I know the places that have known my footsteps and yours will also know theirs, I am content.*
> *But that, my Cerise, is now in your hands. I am too ill to come to Versailles. I cannot speak to your cousin Romain myself. But I have enclosed a letter to him. He cannot object to you personally as his wife, for a prettier, more charming, more accomplished young lady is not today in France. As for the rest, the money, the land, the house, the furnishings, everything I have, I will gladly guarantee all of it to him if he will agree to unite our family lines into one again. The rest lies with you. Do not disappoint.*
> *Votre Père*

She glanced at the enclosed letter. It was unsealed, so she knew her father had intended for her to read it. As he had explained, it was addressed to Vicomte Lévesque and, in her father's grandiloquent style, it spoke of the long, honorable history of their mutual ancestors and how Romain's blood, being from the cadet branch of the family, might well be enriched by marriage to Cerise.

It was an old proposition, one that had been discussed at great length after Cerise's mother died and the likelihood of a son for the house of Bélanger had ended. Romain's father, Paul Lévesque, had considered the offer, but there had never been a formal agreement. Both he and Cerise's father had assumed there was time to spare to betroth their still-young children.

Then Romain's father had died, and Romain succeeded him. At that point, the young vicomte announced that he was disinclined to make any such decision about his future. Despite his mother's urging, he would neither accept nor decline the offer. "Time enough to think of such somber matters," he'd replied, "after I tire of life's diversions."

Over the past three years, Cerise's father had thought it best to let the matter lie, but Romain was twenty-two now and displayed not even a hint of interest in his future. No doubt his mother despaired that he would ever marry and produce an heir.

Cerise clutched her father's letter against her heart. Perhaps he had waited because now was the time. Now was the time she needed him to be ready to marry. And—*Please, God!*—she needed him to be ready to marry her. Before Papa . . .

"Thérèse!"

She hurried to her dressing table and flung open her jewel case. She did not have much in the way of fine jewels, but what she had was of good quality. Rich, but not overbearing. All of it had been gifts from her father to her mother, and her father had exquisite taste in such things.

"Thérèse!" she called again, and her maid bustled into the room with an armful of sheeting.

"Yes, yes, chérie, here I am. If you expected a greyhound, you should not have called for a tortoise."

Cerise spared her only an impatient glance and then went back to her jewels. "I need to look my very best tonight. Papa . . ." Again she clutched his letter. *I cannot live to see another harvest*, he had written before. Now the time was ever so much shorter. Perhaps tomorrow. Perhaps even tonight. *Oh, Papa.* "Papa has written to me that his physician says he has not much time now."

Thérèse's expression was all sympathy. "Oh, my poor petite, I am sorry. But have we not expected this some while now?"

Her lips trembled into a smile, and she blinked back tears. "It was never certain before. Now I must do what needs to be done." She sat at the table, turning her head to one side and then the other, examining her reflection for the slightest flaw. "I must make certain to be presented to Vicomte Lévesque this very night. It can wait no longer. And he has to like me." She turned to her maid and grasped both of her hands. "He *must* like me."

"Shh, shh, shh," Thérèse soothed. "Of course he will like you. How can he not?" She turned Cerise so she was again facing the looking glass. Then she took the fine string of pearls from the jewel case and draped them at Cerise's throat.

"Your dear maman wore these to her wedding, and your papa could not take his eyes from her."

"But Maman was—"

"Not even a jot lovelier than you, chérie, and she was a great beauty in her day. Now, if indeed you must have this popinjay for your husband, we shall make sure you catch his eye this very night."

Thérèse put down the pearls and began unpinning Cerise's hair. Cerise frowned at her in the glass.

"What do you mean, *if* I must? It is Papa's dying wish. Besides, I must marry someone. Who better than he?"

Thérèse held up both hands in surrender. "Who am I to say? My husband was certainly no great lord nor anything much else but a man of his hands. But I would not have traded him for this very palace, I can promise you that."

Cerise huffed. "Because you both lived on Papa's estate in our very home. I daresay you would think quite differently if you had to live in some hovel in the forest and scrounge for firewood and have nothing to eat in the winter but old turnips and watery gruel."

Thérèse laughed. "And where have you heard such tales, chérie? Yes, there are some who live in such a way, far too many, mind you, but that is not the fate of everyone who is not nobly born. There are many who have neither title nor wealth and are yet quite content."

"Perhaps," Cerise allowed, not at all convinced. "But it is likely they have never known anything better."

She remembered how, only that morning, she had given a discarded silk neck ribbon to the girl who tended to the fire. The ribbon was nice enough, but Cerise had never liked the color, a shade of apricot that did nothing for the rosy tones of her skin. Still, the little ash girl had positively bubbled with delight to know it was actually her own. Cerise had made sure to wrap it in a piece of cloth before putting it into the girl's ash-blackened hands.

Cerise looked at her own soft, white hands and then looked at herself in the glass once more. How could she possibly bear it, fetching and carrying, day in and day out? Cleaning and scrubbing until her skin was raw and her back bent and her face lined with care?

She put one hand to her cheek, imagining what it might be like to live in such circumstances. She had seen it often enough. Even as sheltered as she was, she had seen it in the faces of the women who stood aside to let her carriage pass, women who looked well past the age of childbearing, but who had little ones hanging from their skirts. They were hard-faced, worn with the toil of keeping themselves and their little ones fed, warm, and alive from day to day. Young but already old.

With a determined lift of her chin, she met Thérèse's reflected gaze. "I must be introduced to Vicomte Lévesque tonight."

5

Palace of Versailles, France
May 1789

For the next several hours, Cerise suffered through Thérèse's efforts to prepare her for the grand ball that evening. She felt certain she would be black and blue all over the next day after being so pinched and bound and laced. But there was quite a stir among the men present when she appeared in the ballroom in pale blue silk with silver lace and her hair innocent of powder.

The duchesse took her arm the moment she spied her. "There you are, bonbon. How lovely you look. The gentlemen will be positively rioting over you."

Cerise blushed faintly. "There is only one gentleman I hope to bring to such a state."

"Ah, yes," the duchesse said, one eyebrow nearly lost in her powdered wig. "You've not yet met your little vicomte, eh? I will certainly see you are introduced."

Cerise stood on tiptoe, trying her best to see over the heads of all the lords and ladies around her. "He is here, is he not?"

"Oh, certainly, certainly. He returned to court but today, and he is never one to miss one of Her Majesty's fêtes. Do not be obvious, bonbon, but look over there where the archbishop is standing. You have met him, yes? Very good. Now look a bit left of there and you will see the Duc d'Orléans, the Comte de Joubert, and talking with them is Vicomte Romain Lévesque. Now what do you think?"

Careful to not give herself away, Cerise lifted her head and, smiling, scanned the room. There was the archbishop as the duchesse had said. And there, to the left, was the duc, talking to a young man. Her heart sank.

The young man was built a bit like a bulldog, short, bandy-legged, and broad in the chest. His eyes were a pale, watery blue, his lips heavy, and his mouth uncommonly wide. She'd once had a storybook with a drawing of a conclave of forest creatures, and she couldn't help being reminded now of the great, sad-eyed toad who wore a lace ruff and a tricorne hat.

She drew a deep breath and turned to the duchesse, forcing a hopeful smile. "He's . . . not very tall, is he?"

The older woman knit her brow, frowning, and then peered in the bulldog's direction.

"Oh, no, no, no," she said with a sudden laugh. "Not *that* young man. The other one. In the cherry-colored coat."

Cerise looked again. Standing a little to one side of the duc and his toad-like companion was another young man, this one taller than the first though hardly half as broad. His red coat was patterned with gold stripes made up of lines of tiny embroidered oak leaves, and his cravat was so frothy with lace, she wondered how he managed to turn his head or look down at his high-heeled shoes. He leaned close to the duc and said something obviously confidential, and then he threw back his head and laughed, a rather high-pitched, nasal laugh more suited to a boy of twelve than a man fully grown. But he had a pleasant enough face, even if at present it looked a trifle silly. It didn't matter. Soon Sauveterre would be his, and for Papa's sake, she had to make certain she was his as well.

She put her hand on the duchesse's arm. "Introduce us."

"La, bonbon, we are eager. Very well then, come along. I daresay you'll not find a more pleasant young man in all the court."

They made their way across the crowded room, navigating past chattering ladies and gentlemen and servants bearing food and drink. When they were behind the duc, the duchesse boldly tapped his shoulder with her fan.

"Ah, Madame la Duchesse," he said when he turned to see her smiling up at him. "Good evening, and who is this enchanting creature you have with you?"

"Have you not met?" the duchesse asked, feigning surprise. "This is Mademoiselle Cerise Bélanger. Bonbon, this is Monsieur le Duc d'Orléans."

Cerise gave him a demure smile and a slight curtsy. "Good evening, monsieur. It is a great honor to meet you."

"Surely you have heard mention of the daughter of the Vicomte Proulx," the duchesse added.

The duc kissed Cerise's hand, a twinkle in his eye. "I had not, and I see that was my very great loss. But I am certain it is an even greater loss for these two young jackanapes here. Armand. Romain. Here is a pretty cure for your ennui, is it not? Mademoiselle, my godson, Armand Lambert."

The shorter of the young men bowed over her hand. "Mademoiselle."

"And allow me to present Vicomte Romain Lévesque."

The other man made a flourishing bow. "Ah, my little cousin. How very delightful to meet you at last. And even more delightful to see you are not an offense to look at, as are so many of our country-bred demoiselles." He laughed again his giddy, childish laugh, and then took her arm, drawing her away from the others. "Come now, pretty cousin, you must dance with me. You cannot, after so promising a beginning, disappoint me by not dancing like the wind in the aspen leaves. I pray you all will excuse us."

"Please, monsieur." She tried again her prettiest smile, slowing before they reached the other dancers. "My father sent you a message through me. Will you not read it?"

"Here?" Romain asked. "Now? The gavotte is about to begin."

"If you please." She looked up at him through long lashes. "It is such a very little letter and will take hardly a moment to read."

She took the paper from her sleeve and gave it to him.

He frowned at it. "What is it?"

"That is for you to say. If you will have the kindness to read it."

With a bit of a smirk, he opened the message and began reading. He was smiling by the time he looked up from it.

"Ah, I do remember something of this. My dear maman was quite eager for us to make a match, if I am not mistaken."

Cerise nodded encouragingly. "Then you agree it would be the wisest thing to do. After all, it would be a pity if Sauveterre was not passed down to the heirs of my father, would it not?"

"Oh, indeed. Indeed." He gave the message back to her. "But such is the law, ma belle, and Madame le Droit can be quite a harsh mistress."

Her face fell. "Do you not understand, monsieur? It is my father's wish, and your mother's as well, that you make it possible."

"Yes, I see that. Of course. Oh, but it is such a tedious matter, do you not think so?" He took her arm and led her into the throng of dancers. "And have we not many more pleasant things we might be doing this evening?"

Waiting only a moment to hear the rhythm of the music, he swept her into a turn.

They danced three times after that. In between, he introduced her to this gentleman and that, refusing to allow any of them to take his place as her partner. One man, however, refused to be denied.

"Have you not monopolized mademoiselle long enough?" Smiling coldly at Romain, the Comte de Therin-Toussant took her arm before her cousin could whirl her into another dance. "You will pardon me, I am sure. There are so many present tonight who might not bore her. Surely it would be a crime to keep her from them."

"Oh, to be sure, Monsieur Dariole." Romain made an elaborate bow, glancing pointedly at the comte's coattails with the faintest hint of a smirk on his face. "To be sure."

Cerise looked at the comte, startled at the raw fury she saw in his dark eyes. But it was gone so quickly, she almost thought she had imagined it. His eyes cold and hooded, Gaspard bowed in return and guided her into the minuet. At the end of the dance, the queen summoned him, and Cerise hurried back to Romain.

"Oh, no, no, ma belle, let us not speak of serious matters again," he protested when she approached him. "Surely this is too merry a company for such things. Merry, I would say, apart from Monsieur Dariole there with Her Majesty."

There was such a gleam of mischief in his eyes that she could not suppress a smile. "I think, my cousin, you have been very naughty. And why is it you call him Dariole? I dared not ask him, but is that not a pastry?"

Romain laughed. "Maman tells me I shall never grow up, and what do you think? She is right."

"Monsieur?"

"I could not help myself, I promise you. We were at supper a month ago, with all the court, mind you, and he stood to toast the queen. Well, I was very naughty, as you say, and slipped a plate of darioles onto his chair just as he sat again. He looked as if he might be angry, but the king himself laughed, scolding me as he did. What could Monsieur le Comte do but put a brave face on it and laugh as well?"

"Oh, monsieur! It is a wonder he did not call you out over it."

"Over such a trifle? Nonsense. It was merely in jest. Monsieur and I have had many such pleasantries between us. How very bored he would be without them."

She gave him a faint, puzzled smile. "I suppose it will take me some while to grow used to the ways of the court. I cannot think you—"

"Ah, Mademoiselle Cerise Bélanger." The queen promenaded by on the arm of the Duc d'Orléans, fluttering her fan before her powdered face. "And you dance yet again with the Comte Lévesque? He will think you have designs upon him, petite, and upon his title." She looked coyly at the duc. "You would not think our little country mouse would be so ambitious after less than a week here at our court."

She clicked her tongue in teasing reproof, and the duc laughed.

"Alas, my queen," Romain said lightly, "my kinsman, the Vicomte Proulx, has very specifically asked me to look after his daughter. It is such a pleasant task that I am loath to leave it."

Cerise pulled her hand from his and made a quick curtsy. "If you will pardon me, Your Majesty?" With a nod from the queen, Cerise scurried away, weaving through the crowd, making her way as directly as she could toward the doors that opened out onto the terrace. Inside the ballroom, torches and candles and the press of bodies had made it stifling hot. But outside there was a touch of a breeze to cool her burning cheeks. She hurried to the marble railing that overlooked the garden and held onto it with both hands as she took deep, calming breaths.

Her very first royal ball and she had made a spectacle of herself—badly enough to be noticed and teased by the queen. She had scarcely met Vicomte Lévesque, and she was already ruined.

"Ruined!"

"Surely not, mademoiselle."

With a gasp, Cerise turned to see Alexis Dieudonné, the comte's valet, standing in the shadows of the trees. There was again a touch of humor in his dark eyes.

She put one hand over her mouth, realizing she had spoken aloud. Then she drew herself up straight and gave him a disdainful look. "Does your master know you are lurking in the shadows here, monsieur? Idle, rather than seeing to your duties?"

He bowed deeply. "Even the lowliest of slaves is allowed a moment's leisure from time to time, is he not? I did not think I would inconvenience anyone here. Surely there is moonlight enough for us both."

She pursed her lips. The insolent dog was mocking her. Head high, she turned back to the railing and stared into the dark shadows cast by the thick bushes around the fountain, waiting for him to withdraw.

He did not.

Finally she faced him again and fixed him with as icy a glare as she could manage. "Did you wish something? Or do you mean to stand staring all evening?"

The corner of his mouth twitched. "Is it not said that even a cat may look upon a queen?"

"And the queen likely has impudent dogs whipped."

She started to flounce past him, but he reached out one hand, almost touching her but not quite daring.

"Truly, mademoiselle, I did not mean to offend you. I would not have spoken at all, but you seemed to be despairing. Truly it cannot be so grave as that."

Her cheeks burned again. "I do not know what you mean."

"When you said you were ruined. A young lady of beauty and noble blood in the very favor of our gracious queen herself, ruined? How can that be?"

"It . . . there was . . ." She merely shook her head. "It is enough to say that I am *not* in the favor of our gracious queen, monsieur, and it is most likely I will never again be."

6

Cabot Falls, Vermont
Present Day

Sofia smiled as she covered the backdrop with green paint. The forest in Neverland would be lush and verdant, a delight to the eye and to the imagination. She smiled too, listening to Kenny and Luke talking as Luke built a simple frame for another piece of scenery.

"Do you get to build a lot of stuff?" Kenny asked, handing Luke a nail.

"Sure," Luke said, making swift and sure use of his hammer. "All the time. I mean, my dad and I do."

Kenny glanced at Jim and then shrugged a little. "Do you think he might let me try to build something? I mean, only for a couple of minutes. Mom'll be back in a second, and then I'll have to get back to rehearsal."

"I guess." Luke looked up. "Hey, Dad, can Kenny help me with sorting out all the pieces we already cut?"

Jim looked down from the scaffold. "If he wants. Hi there, Kenny."

"Oops." Luke turned to Kenny. "Kenny, that's my dad, Mr. Parker. Dad, this is Kenny."

Jim chuckled. "Yeah, I figured. Good to meet you, Ken. You ever do much woodworking?"

"Not really. It looks kinda fun though."

"Well, you help Luke sort out all the pieces, and later on I'll show you how to put them together. How'd that be?"

Kenny nodded, looking as if he'd been offered a trip to an all-you-can-eat pizza place.

"Both of you be careful," Sofia said with a surreptitious wink at Jim. "No horsing around with the heavy stuff, okay, Luke?"

"Yeah, Mom."

The boys sorted through all the pieces Jim had cut and labeled the night before in the garage. Luke seemed to have a pretty good handle on what needed to go where, and Kenny asked a lot of questions about how it would all work. Sofia's thoughts drifted back to Cerise Bélanger and Alexis Dieudonné until a huff of displeasure drew her back into the present.

"Kenny." Naomi stood at the side of the stage, hands on hips, mouth in a tight line. "Everyone is waiting for you. You've got sawdust on your pants. Dust yourself off and hurry up."

Eyes on the floor, Kenny dusted off his knees. Luke frowned and busied himself with sorting out the variety of screws that would be used on the braces of the backdrops.

Naomi glanced at Jim and then gave Sofia a tight smile. "Have you seen my notebook? It's red and says 'Director' on the cover. It has all my contact numbers in it. I can't imagine what happened to it."

"I haven't." Sofia laid down her paintbrush and wiped off her hands. "Have you, Jim?"

"Not that I remember. Maybe the janitor found it when he was cleaning up last night."

Naomi pursed her lips. "I will ask him about it next time I see him. I'd better get back to the children."

Before she could return to the front of the stage where the kids were milling around, trying to find their places for the first scene, a tall, stoop-shouldered man well past middle age shuffled in through the back door and, with only a grumble, went into the closet-size office marked "Janitor." A minute later, he shuffled back out, bucket in hand.

"This ain't a trash can."

Sofia lifted her eyebrows. "Excuse me?"

"I said this ain't a trash can. It's my mop bucket. Trash cans are clearly marked. If you people have to tear up my auditorium night in and night out, you might at least clean up after yourselves."

Jim smiled at him. "We'll try to keep things as tidy as possible, Mr. Trumbull. Sorry for the inconvenience."

With another grumble, the janitor turned and emptied the bucket into the large receptacle labeled "Trash." Sofia saw a flash of red and immediately put down her paints and brush.

"Hold on. What's that?"

With palpable disdain, Mr. Trumbull retrieved the notebook, holding it by one sodden corner. It had evidently been doused in water and left in the janitor's office. Though the black ink on the cover had bled, the word "Director" was still legible.

"My notebook!" Naomi strode up to the janitor. "Where was it? Oh, it's ruined!"

She snatched it out of Mr. Trumbull's hand.

He merely sniffed. "If you'll be good enough to use the proper trash receptacles, ma'am, I will thank you."

With that, he walked back into his office and shut the door.

Naomi huffed and then noticed her son still standing next to Luke. "Do either of you boys know anything about my notebook?"

Both boys shook their heads.

Naomi frowned. "All right, Kenny, back to rehearsal now. You've bothered Mr. Parker enough."

Kenny looked at the stack of lumber with a sigh. "Sorry, Luke."

Luke shrugged. "That's all right. Dad and I can take care of the rest."

Naomi pursed her lips only the slightest bit. "Go on out front, Kenny, and run through the lines with Megan on this next scene. I'll be right there."

Kenny trudged across the stage and joined the other actors.

Naomi turned to Luke, her expression very sweet. "Would you excuse us for a minute? I need to talk to your mom and dad."

Luke glanced at his parents and then nodded. "Sure. I'm going to get a drink out of the cooler, Mom."

"Just one," Sofia cautioned lightly as Jim climbed down from the scaffold.

"Okay," Luke sprinted off toward the back of the auditorium, and Sofia looked questioningly at Naomi.

Naomi's tight little smile silently seemed to say, *I really don't want to be unpleasant, but . . .* "Kenny seems to be back here a lot," she said aloud. "I hope he's not being a nuisance."

"Not at all." Jim stuck his screwdriver into the loop on his belt. "I don't guess he gets much of a chance to work with his hands, does he?"

"No, not really. It never occurred to me that he might be interested in woodworking. Maybe I can enroll him in a class this summer." Naomi made a note on her clipboard. "But really, when he's here at rehearsal, he needs to keep his mind on his acting, don't you think? I mean, instead of bothering you."

"He's really no bother," Jim assured her. "And it's pretty common at his age to want to be in the middle of everything and know how everything works."

Naomi glanced up at the scaffolding. "I don't want him getting hurt. He doesn't know anything about tools."

"We'll keep an eye on him," Jim said, putting an arm around Sofia's shoulders. "Won't we, hon?"

She smiled. "Sure. Jim's used to keeping track of our four when he's working on something. One more won't be a problem."

"I think it might be best if you . . . discourage him from getting involved backstage," Naomi told her. "Next time the school puts on a play, maybe he can be part of the crew. This time, though, he does have plenty to keep him busy *onstage*, don't you think?"

Sofia nodded. "I'm sure he does. We'll bear that in mind."

"I don't suppose either of you saw anyone with my notebook earlier."

Sofia shook her head. "I'm sorry. I can't imagine who would have done such a thing."

"It was probably only a prank, though I'll have to make sure the children know this is unacceptable." Naomi strode out onto the stage. "All right, Kenny. Megan. Let's go through that scene with the blocking we talked about. Davy? I want you and Caroline to pay attention in case one of you needs to fill in."

Jim went back to his toolbox, but Sofia stood watching them for a moment before she went back to her painting.

"It's funny, isn't it?" she asked.

Jim looked up, tape measure and pencil in hand. "What's that? Her getting a stocking full of coal?"

Sofia giggled. "No, but every time Naomi tells Kenny to do something, he pretty much drags his feet. On the other hand, Davy is all eyes and ears, like he can't wait to get onstage."

Jim chuckled. "Well, Naomi is Kenny's mother. You know it's totally uncool to show any interest in what your mother wants you to do, right?"

"Ah, yes, of course," she replied. "Still, I wonder if he would have gotten the lead role if he weren't her son."

"The question is," Jim said, coming up beside her, "whether he would have even auditioned if he weren't her son."

"True, I suppose. Though from what I've seen, he seems to be a pretty decent little actor. I guess either of them would be good in the part. Davy's just a lot more eager about it."

"Well, Naomi's the director. I suppose she has her reasons. Davy'll be fine as one of the Lost Boys." He picked up his plans and stuck them in his back pocket. "And if it happens, he'll be fine as Peter Pan too. When I was a kid, we didn't have understudies. You knew pretty well you'd better not get sick or break an arm before opening night."

She shook her head. "Get back to work, Hamlet."

He struck a dramatic pose, staring into space. "Is this a hammer which I see before me, the handle toward my hand?"

She pursed her lips, trying not to smile. "That's Macbeth, not Hamlet. Sort of."

"You know, theater tradition says you're not supposed to say the name of—"

"Quiet, you." She laughed and lightly shoved his shoulder. "Just go."

He held up his hands in surrender. "All right, all right, I'm going." He gave her a quick peck on the cheek. "Don't let it get to you. Sure, Naomi's a bit of a trial, but it's not easy keeping a production like this on track, especially with half the cast wishing they were anywhere but here. Some of those Lost Boys obviously aren't here voluntarily. She has her hands full enough without Kenny going AWOL on her all the time."

"You mean Jason and Connor? You don't think one of them might have been responsible for ruining that notebook, do you?"

Jim shrugged. "Hard to say."

"I don't know why they're here anyway," Sofia said, "but I guess it was better than the debate club. At least here they don't have to actually think about what they're going to say."

"Hey, Mom?"

Sofia started, realizing Luke was right behind her. "Don't do that!"

He grinned at Jim and then looked at her with big, innocent

eyes. "I was trying to keep quiet while they're rehearsing."

She put her hands on her hips. "Yeah, right. What is it?"

"I was only wondering if I could come back now."

"Sure. Go help Dad, and make sure you don't leave any mess."

"I know, I know. Mr. Trumbull gets grouchy. He's always grouchy."

"It's part of his job description. Now get going."

Jim and Luke climbed up onto the scaffold, and Sofia went back to her painting. She let her mind wander from present-day Vermont to the Palace of Versailles at the end of the eighteenth century.

The last she had read, Cerise was preparing to go to the royal ball. Sofia tried to envision Cerise, dressed in all her finery, meeting Romain for the very first time. If Cerise had ended up married to an aristocrat, perhaps he was the one. Sofia knew that especially among the nobility, marriage was historically a business arrangement about property and money, and it had little to do with the feelings of the bride and groom. Still, she couldn't help wondering if Cerise and Romain had fallen in love at that first meeting as their hands touched in the minuet. No matter what else she had to do, Sofia was definitely going to read more of the diary before she went to bed.

With a sigh, she dipped her brush into a soft shade of silvery white and began to paint stars.

7

Palace of Versailles, France
May 1789

"You must not think so." The valet's voice was very gentle, not at all mocking as he stood in the semidarkness of the terrace.

Cerise looked up at him once more.

"You must not think you are out of Her Majesty's favor," he said. "Whatever you have done, it cannot be so bad as all that." He glanced toward the doorway that led back into the ballroom. "There's none of them who has not made a false step or two in that rather tricky dance of the courtier. But what? A pretty word here, a touch of flattery there, and you are once again in the sunshine of royal favor. Trust me, I beg you, and do not be like Monsieur Plume de Canard who came to a royal banquet wearing a coat precisely the wrong shade of mustard yellow and could only atone for it with a bullet to his brain."

He pointed two fingers to his temple and gave her such a regretful look that she couldn't help a faint giggle.

"You have made that up."

There was that little glint again in his eyes. "Perhaps, mademoiselle, perhaps. But there is truth in it all the same. You must not permit a little mistake to make you believe all is lost, not when favor is such a fickle mistress. I may be only a valet, but I have seen what it is like, time and again. Tell me now, what is it you have done that is so ruinous?"

She studied him for a long moment, knowing very well that she should not even be speaking to him. *A valet? Papa would likely threaten him with whipping if he knew of it.* And yet there was warm kindness in his velvet-brown eyes along with what seemed to be genuine interest. Oh, she had to speak before she burst! "You are well acquainted with the ways of the court, are you not? If one has offended Her Majesty, how might it be made right?"

"Ah, I see. And have you done so?"

She bit her lip and nodded so that she wouldn't have to risk letting him hear the tears in her voice.

"And how has this happened? Surely you could not have done anything to cause offense."

"I was merely speaking to Vicomte Lévesque and dancing with him. Her Majesty said I was ambitious and had designs upon him and his title."

He lifted one dark brow. "And do you?"

She did. Of course she did, but it seemed so . . . *indelicate* when put in such plain terms.

Her face turned hot once again. "We were merely talking and dancing. Papa sent a message for him through me. It was no more than that."

He considered for a moment. "It seems little enough, mademoiselle. Are you certain Her Majesty truly was offended? It may be she was merely jesting with you."

"I cannot say. She did not seem angry, but I felt I had somehow done something I should not." She took an unsteady breath. "How does one know, monsieur? How does one live in such a place and know how to tread so as not to offend?"

"Truly, that is the great question. In the court of our glorious king and queen, there are little webs everywhere. If one is careful to avoid this one, she may very easily fall into that one. If she avoids both, there is always yet another waiting to trip her up.

The only wisdom I can give you is to be wary of everyone." He glanced around and then turned back to her, his expression suddenly intense. "More than anyone, be wary of my master. He is very used to having what he wants—*who* he wants, even if it is for only a brief while."

Her eyes widened, and her blood coursed a little faster through her veins. She asked him for no explanation. She needed none. She already knew this about the comte. She had felt it in each touch of his hand and had seen it in every covetous look he had turned her way.

When she made no reply, he glanced back toward the ball-room, his expression softening. "And how do you enjoy the ball? A grand occasion, is it not?"

"Oh, it is most wonderful. Everything is so beautiful and the company so merry."

"They very well might be merry," he said, a touch of wryness now in his tone. "So long as they do not think too much on how many of the poor might be fed through the winter for the cost of their merriment."

She drew back from him. Of course it was all the talk, how these radicals demanded that the extravagances of the court be reined in and the money spent on bread for the peasants, but she had not much thought of it herself. She remembered the red, white, and blue cockade he had hidden in his waistcoat pocket. Was he truly willing to kill for his revolutionary ideas?

"I would rather more expect to hear such talk in the streets of Paris than in the king's own palace." She eyed him suspiciously. "And are you one of those who would rebel against His Majesty?"

He made a slight bow. "Oh, no indeed. Their Majesties may be a trifle unacquainted with the world in which their poorer subjects live, but in that I have not found them to be any different from anyone else in their station. I merely think a day may come when they regret their excesses."

"You should mind your tongue, monsieur," she said warily. "You walk very near treason with such words."

"I beg your pardon, for never would I willingly tread such a path." He glanced again toward the music and laughter coming from the ballroom. "But I have found that if a man is made desperate enough, even the most loyal will rebel. I pray Their Majesties need never learn that for themselves. Especially if, by taking a wiser course, such rebellion might be avoided."

She took a step back from him and found herself against the marble railing. He was between her and the door that led back to the ballroom, and she wanted nothing more than to return to the light. Just what sort of a man was he?

"I . . . I should go back now. I will be missed."

He said nothing for a long moment, and he did not step out of her way. Finally, she gathered up her skirts and moved swiftly past him. He caught her arm.

"Have I frightened you?"

She pulled away, giving him only a brief, disinterested glance. "Frightened? Why should I be frightened of a valet?"

His dark eyes shone in the light of the stars. "You think I am dangerous."

"Of course not. I merely—"

"Mademoiselle Bélanger?"

Hearing the voice, the valet made a swift bow over her hand. "Good-night." He melted into the darkness

An instant later, the comte stepped onto the terrace. "There you are. And all alone?"

"It has not been very long," she demurred.

"This is no way to enjoy your very first grand ball, mademoiselle." He brought her hand to his lips, his eyes fixed on hers.

"Shall we enjoy the moonlight together?"

She slid her hand out of his but managed a pleasant smile. "I was rather warm from dancing earlier, but now I believe I am ready to return. Will you accompany me, monsieur?"

There was a twitch of annoyance at the corner of his mouth, but he merely bowed. "I would be honored." He offered her his arm and was accepted. "But I absolutely must have the next dance. I cannot have Vicomte Lévesque take every moment of your time."

"If you like," she said, taking a surreptitious glance toward the darkness where his valet had disappeared. Now there was no sign he had ever been there. "I hope it is a bourrée."

He smiled indulgently. "I will see that it is."

In the following days, Cerise grew more used to the ways of the court. If the queen had been offended by Cerise's attentions toward Romain, she seemed to have forgotten it. Surely the vicomte himself had been no more than amused by Cerise's intention to marry him. Everything, it seemed, no matter how serious, was no more than a subject for his amusement, and he was more often away from court than not.

She frequently saw the valet, Alexis Dieudonné, about the palace. But whether he was about his master's business or involved in something more secret, she did not know. He often looked at her, his dark eyes searching hers, but he was not again bold enough to speak to her.

The comte himself did not miss the opportunity to spend as much time as he was able in the presence of the queen and her courtiers. Her Majesty spent much of her time tending to the little Dauphin, whose illness seemed to grow worse as the spring turned to summer. But from time to time, she came into the garden with her ladies-in-waiting to take the air and refresh herself. They all did their best to assure her that her son would soon be well, and they strove to be cheerful in her presence. The Comte de Therin-Toussant was especially attentive.

He gave Cerise his sly smile as she sat sewing among the other ladies and then bowed before the queen. "Your Majesty, I have come to beg a very great favor of you."

Fluttering her fan, the queen managed a weary smile. "And what is that, Gaspard? Is it outrageously extravagant?"

"I fear it is, Your Majesty. I make myself bold enough to ask the loan of one of your most rare and precious jewels."

She lifted one delicate eyebrow, her expression sobering. "Is that so? And for how long would you have the loan of it?"

"Not long, my queen, unless you would make a gift of it and let it be forever mine."

"Truly, Gaspard, I am fond of you, but this is bold, as you say."

There was a glint of humor in his eye, though Cerise could not tell why. She merely ducked her head and returned to her sewing.

"It is, Your Majesty, which is why I ask only the loan of it for now. For a mere hour or two, no more. And then, upon my life, I swear it shall be returned to you every bit as brilliant and pristine as it was when you lent it me."

The queen pursed her lips. "And why do you want the loan of it?"

"Merely a carriage ride, Your Majesty."

Puzzled by that, Cerise could not help looking up again. She froze to find his eyes fixed on her.

Seeing the sly humor in his expression, the queen laughed. "So *that* is the way of it, eh, Gaspard? By all means, I will loan you this jewel, provided you return it to me precisely as it is now. And then perhaps, one day, we might consider making you a gift of it."

Cerise looked from one to the other, eyes wide. Surely he did not mean . . . surely the queen herself did not mean . . .

She jabbed her needle once again into the silver silk and immediately pricked her finger. "Ah!" She stuck her finger in her mouth for a moment and stood up. "If you will pardon me, Your Majesty, I must see to this before the blood stains the fabric."

She bobbed a swift curtsy. Before she could dart away, the comte grabbed her arm.

"Bind it with this, mademoiselle."

He handed her a lace-edged square of linen from his pocket.

Again she curtsied. "I thank you, monsieur. But I had better let my maid bind my finger. I would not like to spoil so fine a handkerchief as this."

He smiled but did not release her. "I think it has already stopped bleeding."

He took his handkerchief away, and she saw that he was right. Now there was only the tiniest little pinprick on the tip of her finger.

"Rather than risk another such tragedy," he said, tucking her arm into his, "I think you should come with me. Some fresh air will no doubt speed your recovery."

"But Her Majesty—"

"Go." The queen motioned one of the footmen to her. "Go summon this lady's maid."

The footman bowed and hurried off.

The queen shook her head at the touch of annoyance on the comte's face. "If you would borrow one of my jewels, Gaspard, surely you cannot fault me for wanting to keep it safe while it is in your possession."

His mouth twitched at one corner as he bowed before her. "Your Majesty knows me far too well."

Before long, Cerise found herself at the comte's side, driving through the trees. On the seat across from them, Thérèse sat with her hands folded in her lap. Her mild expression covered disapproval only her mistress would have ever detected, but Cerise was grateful for her presence all the same. The comte lounged in one corner of the carriage, fanning himself against the afternoon heat.

"I hear you have even now come from Paris," Cerise said after thinking up and discarding half a dozen other topics of conversation. "My papa always said he would take me there one day."

"You have not been? We must remedy that." The comte took an ornate silver box from his coat pocket and partook of the snuff inside. "But I fear that may be some while from now."

"Yes, of course." She had intended to introduce a topic that would be pleasant and innocuous, something to end the uncomfortable silence, but it seemed in these times there were no such topics.

"The rabble are in an ugly mood," he said, dark eyes brooding. "Some of these so-called 'friends of the people' will be satisfied with nothing but the shedding of every drop of noble blood. They stir up the peasants and drive them to madness and violence against their betters. It is insufferable."

"Perhaps"—Cerise hesitated, remembering what Alexis had told her the night of the grand ball—"perhaps if they were given bread, if they knew that someone saw their needs and was trying to help them, perhaps then they would not be so eager to follow such voices."

The comte's low laugh was not the least bit merry. "Do you think that would help now? All these animals understand is force. If the king shows them the slightest mercy, the slightest weakness, they will turn and tear him to pieces."

She shrank back from him. "Monsieur."

"No, no, now you must not fear. I will see you are protected from such perils. Helpless little girls must be looked after."

She blushed but lifted her chin. "I am not unprotected, monsieur. And my father wishes me to marry Romain Lévesque, Vicomte de Guérin. He will surely look after me."

"Guérin!" The comte laughed heartily, earning a glare from Thérèse. "Well, well. Guérin?" He cleared his throat and put his snuffbox back into his pocket. "Yes, I know about your father's land and title the little coxcomb is to come into one day. But truly, ma belle, he is only a vicomte, and not much of a vicomte at that. It would seem rather a shame for you to throw yourself away on someone who is as well pleased with tavern ale as vintage champagne." He looked her up and down most immodestly. "I, on the other hand, insist on only the very finest."

Her face turned hotter and she looked away from him, saying nothing.

Once more, he laughed. "You may make all the plans you like, and yet the queen may laugh."

She glanced at Thérèse and then looked again at the comte. "My father—"

"This is Versailles, and your father is not the king. Here, especially among her own ladies, our fair Majesty rules. If perchance she might reward one of her courtiers with a favorable marriage, your father is in no position to deny her. Truly, mademoiselle, are you?"

Of course she was not. The queen . . . well, the queen was the queen. It was in her power to dispose of any of her ladies-in-waiting in any manner she found beneficial to herself. Cerise had known that before she came to court, but surely Her Majesty would not do anything hasty. Not when Cerise had been in Versailles for so short a time.

She took a deep breath to slow her racing heart. She would have to continue to win the queen's favor. She fervently prayed Her Majesty would hear her petition about Romain and, for her father's sake, bring about the desired match.

Feeling his eyes upon her, Cerise looked again at the comte. Besides the usual covetousness in his expression, she saw there a touch of smug amusement, as if he held the high cards in a game of faro.

8

Palace of Versailles, France
May 1789

$\mathcal{C}$erise spent the rest of the drive listening to the comte's comments about various courtiers, most of whom she had not met, and how they had either made or ruined themselves at court. She could not help recalling Alexis Dieudonné's tale of Monsieur Plume de Canard and his unfortunate mustard-yellow coat. Perhaps it was not so fanciful a tale as she had first thought. *There are little webs everywhere.*

And yet, she mused, perhaps she should take heed of the comte's tales and accept his help. It was not only he who had told her how swiftly and easily he had won the queen's favor. She had heard it from others in the court. Might he not teach Cerise something of that skill? Then perhaps she, too, might have such success.

Just as they returned to the palace, she gave him her prettiest smile. "How clever you are. I would very much like to hear more."

Then the carriage door opened. Instead of one of the footmen, Alexis Dieudonné was standing at the door. His eyes immediately moved from her to his master.

"Your pardon, monsieur," he said, bowing, "but you wished to wear your new wig to your supper with Their Majesties this evening, and it has not yet been properly fitted. Monsieur Royer has been awaiting your return."

The comte swore and then laughed. "You see, Dieudonné? Even I forget myself in the presence of such beauty as Mademoiselle Bélanger."

Over his master's shoulder, Alexis's eyes flashed to Cerise again. "No doubt, monsieur. Such beauty might make a man forget himself entirely."

She gave him a pleading glance, not sure what he had overheard but certain he would not approve—and certain the opinion of a valet should mean nothing to her. But he was looking straight ahead again, his expression devoid of any emotion at all.

The comte handed her down from the carriage and tucked her arm into his. "Come now. I will escort you and your maid to your chamber. Then I must see to my wigmaker. The queen would be scandalized if I was forced to wear my old one. Go along, Dieudonné. I will be with you presently."

"Certainly, monsieur." Alexis bowed. "Mademoiselle."

Cerise kept her eyes lowered so the comte would not see into her thoughts as she watched Alexis disappear into the palace with a few long strides. In many ways, he was like the comte, tall and dark and lithe. Why could *he* not be the master and his master the valet?

"Mademoiselle?"

She drew a sharp breath and turned her face up to the comte. "Forgive me. What did you say?"

"I said that I would be very pleased to take you for a drive again if you like."

"That would be most agreeable." She clung a little more tightly to his arm. "You tell so many amusing stories of the court. I would greatly enjoy hearing more."

"If that pleases you." He escorted her into the palace and to her chamber, bowing over her hand at the door. "I will attend upon you tomorrow."

She made a deep curtsy and went inside. Thérèse followed like a silent and disapproving shadow.

That night, Cerise tossed and turned, unable to sleep. Nothing was coming together as she had planned. Romain, though always a merry companion, showed not the slightest interest in serious matters. Certainly marriage with her or anyone else was the last thing on his mind. And if what the comte had said was true, the queen herself might give Cerise as a bride to any of her favorites on a whim. *Oh, it would not do! And if Papa dies . . .*

The night was warm and the doors to the balcony were open to let in what breeze there was. She got out of bed and went out to look at the stars to try to soothe her fearful heart. *Oh, bon Dieu.*

She shrank back into the shadows at the low sound of voices. *Is that the comte? No, it is his valet, Alexis Dieudonné, and two other men.* She had seen him only now and again speaking to some of the other servants, the ones who did the menial tasks about the palace—one of the gardeners, the man who shod the horses, one who brought firewood. She had assumed that was somehow a part of his duties for the comte, but now she couldn't help wondering about the little snippet of conversation she had overheard before. *The people will speak, before or after blood is shed.* This was more of the same. Talk of rising up. Talk of the redress of wrongs.

If this valet meant harm to the king and queen, it was her duty to expose him. Then perhaps Her Majesty would be so grateful that she would use her influence with Romain—and Papa could go to his reward in peace.

Before she could think too deeply about what she was doing, Cerise thrust her feet into her shoes, wrapped herself in her cloak, and slipped out into the corridor, certain Thérèse was sound asleep. In a moment more, she was down the stairs and creeping toward the door that led to the part of the garden under her balcony. The door stood open, perhaps to admit the air. Or perhaps it had been left open by Dieudonné.

Keeping close to the wall, she took a silent step forward, listening and hearing nothing. Had they gone already? Her heart was turning circles behind her breastbone, and she was certain her breathing could be heard as far as Notre Dame. But she moved forward still. She was in the dark doorway now. One more step and she would be in the moonlight, visible to everyone, to those cutthroats who plotted on the king's own grounds. One more step.

She bit back a cry as a hand closed on her arm.

"What are you doing?" a low, harsh voice hissed in her ear.

She twisted and squirmed to free herself, but that only made the grip tighten.

"Be still!" the voice hissed. "Be still and quiet!"

She stopped her struggles. At once, the hold on her eased so she could turn around.

"Monsieur Dieudonné. What are you—"

"Shh. Why are you out of your chamber at this hour and without your maid?"

She looked into his dark eyes, eyes that blazed with anger, and wanted to run back to her chamber and hide under her coverlet. Instead, she lifted her chin, her own eyes flashing.

"Are you not afraid to be in the company of such men?" she challenged.

That seemed to startle him. "Which men?"

"Those ruffians. I have heard what they do, these rebels. None of us is safe!"

He shifted on his feet. "I do not think they are so bad as that. True, some of them are rough. Many of them are impatient for things to change. But what they want is not wrong. If you heard some of them speak, if you knew how they long for justice for those who cannot get it for themselves, you might not have so harsh an opinion of them."

She put one hand over her racing heart. "You defend them?"

Alexis looked to his right and then to his left and then behind himself. He lowered his voice even more. "I am one of them."

She gasped. "But it is treason! It is madness! Monsieur, you must not!"

Somehow, despite what she'd heard, she had hoped it was not true. He seemed so intelligent and so kind; how could he possibly ally himself with these villains?

"Shh, shh." He looked around again and then leaned closer to her. "Do you want me to be arrested?"

She covered her mouth momentarily, taking a few seconds to let her breathing slow. "Why? Why would you do such a thing?"

"I have listened to them," he told her, his voice soft but his eyes eager. "They want only what is just and right. Liberty and equality. Too many starve while the court spends on extravagances. How can I stand by and do nothing when I hear their words and know they are true?"

"But they are murderers. They have killed and they have burned! How does such wanton destruction help the poor? How does it make the world more just?"

"No. That is not so. Others have done such things, but not us. And truly, if there are not men like me in such societies, what is to keep those with more radical tendencies from taking over? Should not those who wish for reason and not bloodshed also be heard?"

She looked around, making sure they could not be overheard. "That gardener, the one who limps—"

"You mean Dupont?"

She shrugged, looking around yet again. "I do not know his name. But I have seen—"

"You should not say what you have seen." Alexis's eyes flashed. "I will tell tales of no one but myself. Suffice it to say that a dog may be beaten only so many times before he turns upon his master. And yet, shown only the smallest of kindnesses, he will be forever loyal.

"But this is no hour and no place to discuss such things," he said. "Surely you know what would be said of you if you are seen out alone at night. If you have come to court in hopes of an advantageous marriage, those hopes would certainly be ruined by this. Out at night alone? Anything might happen to you. Even if it did not, what do you think those foolish girls are about when they creep out into the gardens? They are certainly not at their prayers. Perhaps they may find a place as a nobleman's mistress, but never as his wife."

Her face was flaming hot. "You accuse me—"

"Of nothing." He blew out his breath in frustration, and then his expression softened. "Of nothing but forgetting where you are. And who you are." He reached out his hand for hers and then pulled it back, bowing instead. "Forgive me, mademoiselle. I am but a humble servant, and it is not a servant's place to speak so to a lady of the nobility. But still, I beg you, think better what you do."

"Monsieur, I would never—"

"Do not misunderstand me," he said swiftly. "In these perilous times, it is not for your reputation I fear."

"You threaten me?" she breathed, her heart beating even faster than before.

He seized her hands, not allowing her to shrink back from him. "Please. I beg you."

She drew a deep breath, prepared to call for the guard to punish the man for daring to touch her. But something stopped her, something soft and pleading in the dark depths of his eyes, something gentle, something earnest and tender. She exhaled silently. "Let me go."

He released her at once. "I would not hurt you. I swear upon all that is holy, before le bon Dieu himself, I mean only for your good. And I pledge that I mean only for the good of France as well. Please, return to your quarters before either of us is seen."

With only a nod, she turned and fled to her chamber. She should report all of this. She should give someone the names of the men who had been plotting in the garden and tell what she had overheard. But how could she on so little evidence condemn them to prison or even death? The valet, Alexis . . . surely he meant no wrong, not to her or to France. And there *was* much suffering among the poor. Surely one could support the king and yet want some things to be different.

She didn't know what she should think, much less what she should do. Was it worth winning the gratitude of the queen at the price of the life and freedom of a good man? Or was everything Alexis had said to her merely a blind, a way to soften her resolve and keep her from reporting what she had seen?

She would have to find out more.

The comte took Cerise on another carriage ride the next day. As he spoke of his lands and other holdings and the favor he had with Her Majesty, Cerise thought back on her encounter with his valet, on the look in those brown-velvet eyes and whether or not it could be trusted, and what her duty was to France and the king. But when the comte was handing her out onto the steps of the palace, she noticed the gardener with a limp, Dupont, was busying himself with one of the bushes near where one of the grooms stood holding the horses.

She turned her back so he would not realize she had noticed them. Servants were used to being invisible, weren't they?

He spoke only two words, his gravelly voice a mere breath over the restless shifting of the horses and the jingling of the harness. Then he moved along to the next bush, his shears shaping it with effortless perfection. In that same moment, the driver urged the horses forward. The groom at their head walked along with them and out of sight.

But Cerise only smiled to herself. Surely she had not overheard his words for no reason. She would find out whether Alexis had been honest with her, and then she would know what she must do. Dupont's two words were all she needed: *Tonight. Stable.*

9

Cabot Falls, Vermont
Present Day

The next meeting of the Pinot Painters was on a blustery, bitter-cold night. But from the warm coziness of Sofia's four-season room, the blue-black night and the stars that twinkled over the snow seemed more romantic than forbidding.

"You know, Marla," Julie said, looking around her canvas so she could grin at Sofia, "you never did tell us how your blind date went."

Marla shrugged. "It was nice."

"Nice?" Sofia asked. "*Nice*? That's it?"

"She means it was hideous," Julie said, pursing her lips.

"No." Marla blushed a little and rinsed the paint from her brush. "Really, it was nice."

"Aaaaaaaand?" Sofia urged.

"At least tell us his name and what you did." Julie opened a new tube of cadmium red paint, more than a hint of mischief in her eyes. "Or tell us to mind our own business."

Marla laughed. "His name was Robert, and do *not* make the mistake of calling him Bob."

Julie snickered.

"Anyway, we finally found a movie we both wanted to see and afterward agreed it was pretty lame. Then we went out into the mall and had some ice cream. That was about it."

Sofia shook her head. "I don't think so. Not judging by the look on your face. Was he a creep?"

"No!" Marla insisted. "I was pretty nervous, but Robert was very sweet."

"So then what?" Sofia insisted. "Tell us everything."

"Yeah," Julie said. "Spill."

Marla bit her lip and laughed softly. "Actually, 'spill' is about right. When we got the ice cream, his elbow bumped into my arm as he was putting his wallet away. My ice cream fell off the cone and onto the front of my shirt. I was so embarrassed. And he turned so red, I was afraid he was going to pass out. He turned even redder when he was trying to help and couldn't decide if he should blot my shirt or simply hand me napkins. By then, his ice cream had melted all over his hand."

"What a great first date!" Julie crowed.

"Poor guy," Sofia said. "Do you think you'll see him again?"

Marla looked into her wine glass. "Probably not. He was very nice and seemed like a decent guy, but that was it. There wasn't really any chemistry there."

"Too bad. I was hoping you'd get a soul mate for Christmas. But I'm glad you went anyway. It's good to get out there," Sofia said. "At least your dating doesn't have political and national consequences like it did back in Cerise's day."

"The poor girl," Marla said. "I don't guess she's going to end up very happy."

Sofia shrugged. "From what I've read so far, it doesn't seem very likely."

"How's it going with your own Marie Antoinette—the play director? Has she ordered anyone to be beheaded yet?"

"That was the Queen of Hearts," Sofia said, laughing. "And Marie Antoinette wasn't as bad as people think she was. But she was so out of touch with her people, she didn't realize that what she was doing was making them hate her."

"Hmm." Marla pursed her lips. "Sounds like Madame Director, if you ask me."

Sofia sighed and went back to her painting. There was another rehearsal to get through tomorrow.

As she pulled her Suburban into a space in the auditorium parking lot the next day, Sofia cringed inwardly. Naomi was parking her Ford in the space right next to her.

Putting on a determined smile, Sofia got out of her car and slung her bag of paints over her shoulder.

"Hello, Kenny. Naomi. I thought I was early."

Naomi glanced at her watch. "A bit. Where's Luke today? I hope he isn't ill or anything."

"Oh no. His dad's bringing him. I had some errands to run, so I came straight here. I thought I'd get a chance to finish painting the mermaid lagoon today."

Naomi nodded. "We wanted to run over some lines before everyone else got here, didn't we, Kenny?"

The boy nodded, squirming a little. "Don't we need to wait for Megan and some of the other kids?" he asked.

"I'll fill in," Naomi said brightly, her clipboard and new notebook clutched in her arms. "Now, come along."

Sofia followed them inside

"Kenny?" Naomi said. "What's this?"

Kenny trudged over to his mother, who was standing in front of the stage. Shifting her bag from her shoulder to her arms, Sofia followed. There at center stage was the Peter Pan costume, green tights, feathered hat and all, torn to shreds.

Kenny's eyes were wide. "I . . . I don't know, Mom."

He looked at Sofia, bewildered.

"I thought you were supposed to take it home and try it on last night," Sofia said.

"Yeah, I was supposed to." He squirmed guiltily. "I guess I forgot."

"But I thought you had it," his mother said, hands on hips. "After all the work Mrs. Hendrickson put into making that for you, and you let this happen to it? You *forgot*?"

"I didn't totally forget, Mom. I put it in my backpack, honest. Then I forgot to take it out and try it on. But it was in my backpack."

"Where did you have your backpack after you put it in there?" Sofia asked, trying to be as gentle as possible. "Was it with you all the time?"

"Yeah." He bit his lip. "Except when we were rehearsing. I stuck it under the bench that's backstage so it'd be out of the way."

"So, nearly anybody could have gotten into it." Sofia glanced at Naomi and then turned back to Kenny. "Did you open your backpack at all last night or earlier today?"

He shook his head. "I threw it on the chair in my room like I always do. I was going to do my homework after rehearsal. I didn't even bring it with me today."

Naomi pursed her lips. "All right, Kenny. Sit down over there until everyone else gets here. We're going to work on Scene Six, so please go over your lines."

"Yeah," he mumbled. He picked up a script from the table in the corner and sat down in one of the front-row seats, head down and shoulders slumped.

"It's really not his fault," Sofia said. "Anybody could have gotten it out of his backpack."

She climbed the steps to the stage with Naomi following close behind. Both of them looked down at the ruined costume.

"Now what?" Naomi asked after a moment. "Stephanie has more work than she can do already without having to redo this."

"I don't suppose it could be mended." Sofia picked up the green tunic and it fell in ribbons back on top of the ruined tights. "Guess not."

With a huff, Naomi jotted down a note on her clipboard. "She'll have to make time somehow. It will be opening night before we know it."

"She really does have her hands full, especially with her new baby. I don't know how she gets anything done." Sofia paused for a second. "Listen, my sisters are both excellent seamstresses, and they're coming to visit for Christmas. I bet if I were to ask them nicely and make them almond croissants, they might agree to lend a quick hand. What do you think?"

Naomi looked at her as if there were some kind of catch. "You . . . think they wouldn't mind?"

"All I can do is ask. They're pretty creative with this kind of thing. I'm sure they'd do a great job."

"You know it has to be on a volunteer basis," Naomi reminded her. "We couldn't pay them anything."

Sofia smiled. "I don't think they'd expect it. Not for a school play. But let me talk to them about it before I promise anything." She looked over at Kenny, sitting in the front row, hunched over his script, looking utterly miserable. "We'll get it figured out, okay, Naomi? Things like this happen. You almost have to expect something unexpected when you put on a play. I don't want him to feel bad about it."

Naomi shook her head. "He should have been more careful. I had so much on my mind, I didn't even think to ask him about the costume. I guess it's my fault too."

Sofia dropped to one knee and scooped up the remains of the costume. "We really shouldn't blame anybody except for the person who did this. We need to find out who did it and why."

Naomi pinched the bridge of her nose." I don't have time for this. I really don't have time for this."

"I don't think it's serious." Sofia stood up and stuffed the ruined fabric into her bag. "Not at this point. Not enough to call the police."

"The police! You don't think . . ." Naomi glanced back to see Kenny was listening in and lowered her voice. "You don't think we ought to be worried, do you? I mean, about safety. Really, it had to be one of the children, right?"

Sofia thought of the slashed costume and the obvious anger that had inspired its destruction. *But whose anger?* Sofia knew many of the kids were frustrated with Naomi's strict rules. The woman sure knew how to take the fun out of a project. And some of the kids, particularly the boys, were not voluntary members of the cast. Were they acting out in response to being required to participate? Or was this anger from someone who felt he should have been chosen for a more important role? Or maybe it was more than childish temper and destructiveness. Sofia shook off the thought.

"More than likely it was nothing but a prank," Sofia told Naomi brightly. "We'd better talk to all of the kids before rehearsal starts though. Just to find out if anybody knows anything."

The other woman nodded. "And if you'd talk to your sisters about that costume, I'd certainly appreciate it."

"I'll do that," Sofia assured her.

There was a bustle at the auditorium doors, and the rest of the cast started to arrive. Davy came in through the backstage entrance and joined the others. A few minutes later, Connor and Jason came in the same way. Both of them looked windblown and red-faced, as if they had been outside longer than it took to walk to the building from the parking lot. Both of them looked a little startled to see Sofia watching them.

While Naomi gathered the kids together and began quizzing them about the ruined costume, Sofia slipped outside and had a look around. But all she found there were some old empty crates, the dumpster, and a cold wind.

"Nobody admitted anything, right?"

Sofia's oldest sister, Rosa, frowned as Sofia brought cups and a fresh pot of coffee to the kitchen table where Rosa and their middle sister, Gina, sat. They and their families had arrived in time to help cook dinner and then get settled all over the house.

"Nobody claims to know anything," Sofia said. "Kenny's upset too."

"Poor kid," Gina said. She examined one of the rips in the green tunic laid out on the table. "But we can remake this pretty quickly, don't you think, Rosa? It's pretty simple."

"Sure," Rosa said. "No trouble at all. Jack and Franco are taking the kids out sledding tomorrow. We can do it then."

Sofia smiled, glad they had both been able to take a little time off from their highly technical jobs and visit Cabot Falls for Christmas. "And while you two work, I'll make croissants."

Gina's blue eyes lit. "Sold!"

"Pushover," Rosa said, chuckling. "So," she asked Sofia, "how's everything else going? You're taking excellent care of Nonna's quilt, right?"

Rosa smiled, but Sofia knew her oldest sister was fiercely protective of the family heirloom.

"Of course I am. I keep it out of the light and never, never, *never* touch it with my bare hands. There *was* that time I spilled coffee, though . . ." Sofia watched her sister's eyes widen in horror, so she quickly let her off the hook. "Just kidding."

Gina stifled a laugh, and Rosa gave them both a reluctant smile. "Good."

"Speaking of the quilt," Sofia said, "Nonna used to talk about our ancestor who had escaped from The Terror during the French Revolution and ended up penniless in England. Do either of you remember hearing about that?"

Rosa nodded. "I remember. Nonna always said we should act like ladies because we had noble blood in our veins."

The three sisters smiled at the memory.

"I don't recall her saying anything very specific." Gina frowned. "Not a name or anything like that."

Sofia searched their faces. "But do you remember what her title was? I think I do, but I don't want to twist my memory to make it fit what I want it to fit."

Gina looked at Rosa. "You mean to fit what's written in the diary."

Sofia nodded expectantly.

"I don't know," Gina said. "A duchess or a countess or something. It's been a long time, and the only titles I know about are on the covers of romance books."

Rosa snorted. "Well, what I remember is that she was a countess, but I don't think Nonna ever mentioned her name. Is that what you remember?"

Sofia smiled. "That's what I think I remember. It's been so long since Nonna even mentioned it, I wasn't sure I was remembering right at all."

"So, the girl in the diary," Gina said, "she's a countess?"

"I don't know. Her father was a viscount, but she couldn't inherit that because she was a girl. She must marry into the title of countess, but I don't know who she marries." Sofia sighed. "I'm not even sure if this is the same girl."

"How many countesses do you think we have in the family?" Gina asked, snickering.

Sofia made a face at her. "This girl might not even end up being a countess."

Rosa tapped her pursed lips with one finger. "You know, if Nonna told us about this countess in exile, don't you think it's pretty likely she told someone else?"

"Aunt Rachel and Aunt Louisa!" Sofia said. "They must have heard Nonna's stories about having noble blood when they were little girls too." Sofia leaned over and gave her oldest sister a smacking kiss on each cheek. "Thank you. I'll ask both of them about it."

10

Palace of Versailles, France
May 1789

Cerise waited until she was sure her maid was asleep. Then, as swift and silent as nightfall, she slipped into one of Thérèse's dresses, pulling it as tight as she was able in the back, knowing it practically swallowed her no matter what she did. Well, she would take Thérèse's cloak too. It would cover a multitude of aesthetic sins.

Once dressed, she put her hair into a simple braid as she had seen some of the servant girls do and otherwise left it unadorned. All that was left was to put on her shoes. She could never borrow Thérèse's and hope to walk. Her own would have to do. She would simply have to keep anyone from noticing them and wondering where a simple maid had gotten such finery.

She wrapped herself in Thérèse's cloak and then studied herself in the looking glass one last time. She went to the grate and touched her fingertips to the soot, then rubbed her hands together, only enough to make them look grimy. She rubbed them on her face too. She did not look too dirty, but neither did she look too clean. What was certain was that she did not look as though she were of the nobility.

Her reflection smiled back at her, though the eyes were wide and perhaps a little frightened.

"Nonsense," she hissed at her reflection. "I will merely go

see what he is doing. It is not as if I will be walking the streets of Paris alone at night."

She arranged the cloak's hood so she could no longer see those frightened eyes. She was merely a lady's maid on an errand. That was all. *If Papa ever knew . . .*

But he would not know. No one would. Not unless she waited too late and was caught. Well, she wouldn't think of that just now. She was only taking a little walk in the evening air. That was all.

With the cloak pulled snugly around her, and moving in perfect silence, she slipped out of her chambers. Forcing herself not to run, she made her way to the ground floor by the passages the servants used. She passed several of them as she went, but they were too busy with their own duties to take notice of her.

In the garden she scurried from tree to tree, from shadow to shadow, fearing every sound behind and ahead of her. It was madness to go on. But after risking this much, she could not turn back. Finally she made her way around to the stables. It was not very late yet, and she found no one inside besides a few dozing horses and an old hostler reeking of wine and soiled straw. Certain he would not stir until morning, she crept past him and hid herself in an empty stall, hoping she had not long to wait.

It was no more than a quarter of an hour before Dupont arrived. The groom he had spoken to came in shortly thereafter. She shrank back into the shadows as they made a quick survey of the place, but they did not see her.

"And the others?" the groom asked, his close-set eyes narrowed. "Surely it will take all of us to bring them around."

"Or to silence them entirely."

The groom nodded wolfishly. "But where are they?"

"Patience," said Dupont. "They will come."

The words were scarcely out of his mouth when a third man emerged from the darkness. "Not tonight," he hissed. "Not tonight.

We are suspected. This place is not safe. The others have decided we should go to the rookery. We must meet them there tomorrow night."

The other two nodded, their faces grim.

The man who had brought the warning moved into the faint light of the moon. It was Alexis. All three of them had the red, white, and blue cockade subtly displayed somewhere on their persons. Alexis's was barely noticeable, just peeking out from the edge of his waistcoat pocket.

Cerise had leaned forward to get a better view of the men, wanting to make sure she heard anything else they might say, when something rustled in the straw beside her.

At once, the men turned to the sound.

Dupont seized the pitchfork that leaned against the stable wall. "Who's there?"

She froze where she was, sinking back into the darkness as best she could.

"Who's there, I say!" Dupont swore. "Why is there no light in this wretched place?"

She stayed where she was, her heart racing faster. Alexis took a step forward, his dark eyes glinting as he nodded at the old hostler, still snoring away. "Do not be a fool, Dupont. Old Grand-Père there would likely roast himself alive if he were left with a lantern."

"But there is someone there." Dupont brandished the pitchfork. "Come out or you will taste the tines of this fork."

There was more rustling in the hay beside her. Then someone burst out, throwing himself at the feet of the three men. It was Michel, the gardener's boy.

"Please, monsieur, I meant no harm. I merely fell asleep."

"Polisson!" Dupont growled. "What have I told you about being where you should not? Must I again beat sense into you?"

The boy ducked his head. "No, monsieur, I beg you."

Alexis put one hand on the boy's shoulder. "Wait now, Dupont. Wait. Tell me, Michel, what woke you?"

"I heard Monsieur Dupont asking for light. I thought at first it was part of my dream, and then I knew it was not. Please, monsieur, I meant no harm."

Alexis gave the two men a slight nod. "Go on to your bed, boy, and see you do not fall asleep elsewhere, eh?"

Michel leapt to his feet and bowed repeatedly. "Yes, monsieur. Thank you."

He bolted out of the stable before Dupont could do more than curse at him again.

Cerise held her breath.

"Tomorrow then," Dupont said, evidently satisfied he was no longer overheard.

"Until then," the groom said, and he and his companion disappeared into the darkness.

Alexis watched them go and then slipped out too. Cerise waited a moment and then hurried after him, but already he was out of sight. Suddenly she found she did not much care for being out alone. She wanted only to get back inside the palace, back to her own chamber, back to the comforting sound of Thérèse snoring in her trundle bed.

She darted back around to the gardens the way she had come. The door back into the palace was not a hundred yards away when a hand over her mouth muffled the scream that rose in her throat. An arm went around her waist and lifted her off her feet, dragging her back into the shadow of a clump of trees.

"Quiet," a voice hissed in her ear. "You will give us both away."

With a shudder, she stopped her struggles.

"Alexis," she breathed, stumbling a little when he suddenly released her. "Monsieur, I—"

"Are you *insane*?" he asked, his voice still a low hiss.

"What madness brings you here? And dressed so?"

He plucked at Thérèse's cloak, and she could see the angry glint in his eyes even in the darkness.

She pushed his hand away. "I am loyal to the king and to the queen, monsieur. If others are not, is it not my duty to find out?"

He stuffed the red, white, and blue cockade deeper into his waistcoat pocket, making her certain now that it was indeed a symbol of his secret society.

"This is no place to discuss such things."

"And who is it they spoke of? Who are they to make one of you?"

"That is of no importance. You must come back into the palace before you are seen." He seized her arm and hurried her toward the door. "Do you think you are courageous to do such foolish things?"

She pulled her arm out of his grasp and stalked toward the door. He strode after her, followed her inside, and stood between her and the corridor that would allow her to escape.

"Your actions are childish," he spat, voice little more than a whisper. "Reckless. Foolish!"

"Let me pass."

"Don't you realize your life stood at the point of a knife just now? If the boy had not come forward when he did, there is nothing I could have done to stay Dupont's hand."

"He would not." She shook her head. "Surely he would not." She looked back toward the way she had come, and her heart thudded against her breastbone. "None of them would dare do anything here at the palace itself."

He exhaled heavily. "I wish, for the sake of all who inhabit these walls, that there was better protection. Anyone may come in and out. Yes, there is the Swiss Guard for the king and queen, but they cannot be everywhere at once." His expression became intense. "I beg you, mademoiselle, do not walk out alone." He exhaled, managed a sheepish smile, and bowed again. "I would not for all the world have anything happen to you. May I escort you back to your chamber?"

She pressed her lips into a tight line, her expression flinty. Without another word, she pulled her hood down so it shadowed her face more thoroughly and pushed past him. He followed at a respectful distance until she reached her own door. Then, with a bow, he left her.

Palace of Versailles, France
June 1789

The lavish Salon de Mars was filled with light and music and a throng of nobles gloriously dressed. The king stood, signaling that the ball had officially begun. The queen took his arm, and they began the first of the danses à deux. As was tradition, the ball began with these single-couple dances, first with Their Majesties and then in descending order of rank with the other ladies and gentlemen of the court. It should have been an honor, but Cerise had to force a smile and a pretty acceptance when the comte claimed her hand to partner with him when his turn came.

Though she was thinner now and worn with worry over the worsening illness of her son, the queen made her usual dazzling appearance. She danced like sunlight on water, seeming hardly to touch the ground even in the measured steps of the minuet. Her husband stepped more ponderously, but he seemed content to let the attention fall to his dazzling partner. Blue eyes sparkling, graceful hands moving in time with graceful feet, sweet mouth turned up with pleasure, she was a glorious sight.

Cerise sighed. "Her Majesty dances to make the angels weep with envy."

The comte smiled, not taking his eyes from the sovereign couple. "And you would be wise to tell her so, ma belle. A word here and there would be a fine investment in royal favor."

She ought to be grateful for his guidance, she knew. But truly, was there nothing he ever said or did that was not with an eye for advancement? At least she knew he would not seek her in marriage, if only for that reason. A poor vicomte's daughter? No, she could not add prestige to his name. He desired her—his attentions so far were clear proof of that—but he would never make her an honorable offer. She would certainly accept no other.

And perhaps, in some roundabout way, his attentions and his insistence on bringing her to the queen's notice would make her alliance with Romain possible after all. For that, she gave the comte a grateful smile. At once, his expression turned sly and knowing. He brought her hand to his lips.

"The angels may envy Her Majesty, but truly I believe you are one of their own."

She turned her head, putting up her fan so he could not see the color in her cheeks. But still she smiled, clung to his arm, and listened to his flowery discourse until he was summoned by the queen herself. Cerise took the opportunity to step out onto the balcony.

A moment later, she heard someone call to her from the shadows. She recognized the voice. Ignoring the sudden flutter in her breathing, she turned.

"Monsieur Dieudonné."

The valet stepped only a little way into the light and bowed. "Mademoiselle is having a pleasant evening, I trust."

"I am." She lifted her chin. "Did you come to tell me how to behave myself inside the palace as well as out of it?"

His lips twitched. "Not I, mademoiselle. I merely wished to see that all was well with you."

"It is. Your master has been good enough to favor me with his attentions. It is an honor I am well aware of."

"And mean to use," he said, his face hard as flint.

She pursed her lips and turned, meaning not to give him another moment of her time, but he would not let her go.

"What is it you play at?" he asked. "Do you think my master is to be trifled with?"

She gave him an icy smile. "He has been very helpful to me. He knows the ways of the court, and he knows how to win the favor of the king and queen. I am certain there is much more he can teach me."

"And perhaps that knowledge will come at a price so dear, you will regret having paid it."

"I am certain I do not know what you mean."

"Do you not? Do you fancy yourself some fine coquette?"

She lifted her hand to strike his insolent face, but he caught her wrist, then released it and stepped back.

"Forgive me, I meant no insult to you. I merely would not like to see you taken in by him. You would not be the first he has used and cast off."

There was such concern in his expression, such genuine tenderness in his eyes, that she hadn't the heart to be angry with him.

"I know," she said. "But what else can I do? My papa . . ."

Despite his radical ideas, there was something about Alexis that made her want to tell him everything, about Papa and about Romain and even about his master, the comte. Alexis had not exactly been respectful to her, not always. But when he was not, he was piercingly honest. She felt certain he meant only good by it. At least, unlike when she was in the presence of the comte, she did not feel like cringing each time he looked upon her.

He leaned down a little, trying to look into her downcast eyes. "Please. Tell me. I swear your secrets are as safe with me as if I were your own priest."

She drew a shuddering breath. "My papa is very ill and I fear—"

"Cerise!"

Alexis stepped back into the shadows as the duchesse fluttered out onto the balcony.

"There you are! What are you doing, standing alone in the darkness? I thought you had set your cap at the Vicomte de Guérin. He has arrived, bonbon. Now is the perfect time."

She seized Cerise's arm and hurried her inside.

"Monsieur!" the duchesse called, her voice high and piercing. She pulled Cerise across the room to Romain. "You must dance with Mademoiselle Bélanger. Oh, pardon me, but there is the archbishop."

She pushed Cerise toward him and then wove her way into the crowd.

Romain only looked amused. "I take it mademoiselle would care to dance?"

Cerise made a deep curtsy. "Monsieur honors me."

Soon they were moving through the steps of the dance, stately and gracious, their movements mirrored by the dancers around them. He smiled at the admiring looks they received.

"We do make a fair couple, my little cousin." They turned and then came together again. "Do you not think so?"

She gave him a coy glance and then turned away, still in the figure of the dance. *Oh, Papa, it may still be.* He tended to simper at times, and his interests went no deeper than the latest fashion in cravats, but she supposed there were worse things. Marriage to him might be nothing more than a duty, but she felt sure he would never be deliberately unkind. Indifferent, perhaps, but it did not seem in his nature to be cruel. She returned his smile as they joined hands again.

"It is not my place to say, monsieur. But if what pleases you also pleases my papa, then I, too, am pleased."

He chuckled. "But we must please more than Papa." There was a hint of regret in his expression. "Our lovely queen must have her own way, must she not?"

"I—"

"The dance, petite, the dance."

She realized she had swayed to a stop.

He hurried to catch them up to the rest of the dancers. For a time they were silent, merely following the pattern, and then they were again moving side by side.

He squeezed her hand. "It seems Her Majesty has other plans for her humble servant."

Cerise looked forward, still dancing, her expression a mask of serenity. "Plans?"

"Oh, certainly. You know Madame Plamondon has served the queen and her children long and well. She has a daughter that's recently come of age, and how better to reward the lady's years of service than to find her daughter an agreeable match? It seems she and I are to be married."

11

Palace of Versailles, France
June 1789

"Married?"

Again Cerise turned away from Romain, her steps heavy as she wove through the line of dancers and then met with him again. "And you will agree to this alliance?"

He laughed softly. "We all serve Her Majesty, do we not? I have met the girl a time or two. She is a bit freckled and squints abominably, but she will do as well as another."

Cerise kept her face serene, going through the stately dance mechanically as her mind whirred, scrambling to think of a way to get around this new obstacle. In her short time at court, she had learned that even a queen's plans might be changed.

"And is her mind absolutely made up?" Cerise asked several turns later.

He raised one eyebrow. "Whose mind, little cousin? And about what?"

She gave him her sweetest smile. "Her Majesty's. Is she positively determined that you shall marry this Mademoiselle Plamondon?"

He turned away and then back again in the waning measures of the minuet. "It would seem she is. She has not absolutely commanded it, no, but she has said it would please her. Now, tell me, mon chou, what man who wishes to advance himself in society would even consider refusing his queen's slightest wish?"

Cerise's heart soared as the final chord sounded and he bowed over her hand. Clearly nothing had yet been decided. Sauveterre might still be saved.

"But there has been no formal betrothal?"

"I begin to think your interest in me lies somewhere beyond my many charms." He chuckled, and she realized he was teasing her again.

She made her smile coy instead of letting her impatience show. "Would it be so terrible a thing? To reunite your side of the family with mine? Or perhaps you are fond of squints and freckles."

"Monsieur is fond of leisure and pleasure and not displeasing his queen," he said as he escorted her to a chair. "If you can think of how we may both have what we wish, I would be most happy to avoid the squints and freckles." He shrugged, his expression more indifferent than rueful.

"Perhaps if you spoke to the queen yourself, if you told her it was your wish as well as mine—"

He shook his head. "My mother would have liked you, little cousin. She always told me my idleness would be the ruin of me, but there seems to be nothing idle in your determination or in your single-mindedness. She admired such traits, though she despaired of finding them in either her husband or her son."

Cerise peeped at him over her fan. "But you might, if you choose wisely, find them in a son of your own."

At that, he laughed loudly enough to turn a few heads and draw the attention of the queen herself. But in another moment, the queen had turned back to the noble she was dancing with and was lost in the throng. The comte, however, set down his glass of champagne and made his way to Cerise's side.

"You have a merry companion, mademoiselle," the comte observed. "But then, who would not be merry at the prospect of being wed to the exemplary Mademoiselle Plamondon? Dance with him now, ma belle, for soon he will be off the market."

Romain's eyes twinkled. "Monsieur Dariole, how good of you to pay your compliments." He reached over and gave the comte's coattails a subtle brush. "Or should I say, how sweet? For what, truly, is sweeter than a dariole?"

Cerise covered a giggle with her fan, glad that the comte did not look her way.

The comte made a stiff bow to Romain. "Monsieur is very droll, as always." He took out his ornate snuffbox and, after helping himself, offered it to Romain. "I am certain your wife will find the quality most endearing."

"Merci," the vicomte said, accepting. "You're a good fellow, monsieur, and have excellent taste in snuff."

"I am gratified," said the comte, and then he turned to Cerise. "Will you favor me with the next dance? I believe it is to be a bourrée."

She bowed her head, still suppressing a smile. "Do pardon me, but the vicomte has claimed my next two. Perhaps after that?"

"Of course," the comte said evenly. "Of course. Do excuse me." He kissed Cerise's hand and with one last bow, returned to his champagne.

Cerise turned toward Romain, trying to look stern. "You should not tease him so. It is really too bad of you."

"Is it? I do not think so, my pretty cousin. Monsieur Dariole knows I speak only in jest. He and I are the best of friends always. Now, come let us dance once again."

The next morning, Cerise sat with the queen, her ladies and the comte in the garden. Cerise was sewing tiny golden fleurs-de-lis on silver silk. It was to be the bodice of Her Majesty's new gown, a special request of the queen herself. Cerise was especially careful with each stitch. If she could particularly please the queen, perhaps she would be indulgent when Cerise asked about Sauveterre and would change her mind about Madame Plamondon's daughter and Romain.

"It is exquisite," the queen said, taking her sewing from her and holding it up in the bright sunlight. "I have never seen work so fine."

Cerise curtsied deeply as she took it back from her. "Your Majesty does me much honor."

The queen smiled, showing even white teeth. "It pleases me, chérie, to give favor to those who please me. It seems to me that there is much I might do for you as well."

Cerise ducked her head, trying to hide her excitement. Perhaps it was not so unlikely as she had imagined. "Your Majesty is too kind. I am merely—"

"Of course," the queen continued as if Cerise had not spoken, "you are young and alone. Your father, heaven spare him, may not be with you long. He would, as you have said, most want to see you provided for, and how better than to find you a suitable husband, no?"

"I would never presume—"

"Oh, la, petite, it is a small matter. I will find you a husband, and then you will no longer have to put yourself forward in so vulgar a fashion as you did last night."

Cerise felt the color flame into her face. "Your Majesty?"

"Truly, it was the talk of all the court the way you threw yourself at Vicomte Lévesque. I am certain I was not the only one to notice. Madame Plamondon was quite shocked that you should monopolize him so before her very eyes." The queen's smile was saccharine. "I am certain you must have heard of my plans for her daughter and the vicomte, no?"

Cerise cast her eyes to the ground. "Yes, my queen. I had

heard . . . something of it. I did not know it was already settled."

The queen frowned contemplatively. "Not settled, perhaps. Not yet. But I have told the vicomte it would please me. So truly, what more is there to be said about it?"

The comte stood and made a graceful bow. "I am certain the child meant no disrespect to Your Majesty. She has been at Versailles such a little while yet, and it is obvious that she is ignorant of how these things are done. She merely needs the guidance of someone who knows the ways of the court and of Your Majesty."

"Yourself, Gaspard?" the queen asked with a silvery laugh. "Oh, it is good of you, and she is a pretty little trifle, truly, but—"

"It will amuse me, my queen. And, of course, it will please me to see your plans are not interfered with. The Vicomte Lévesque will do very well with Mademoiselle Plamondon. How could he not? And our little seamstress here, well, perhaps she deserves someone of higher rank than even a vicomte."

"That shall be seen to, Gaspard," the queen said, and she patted Cerise's arm. "All in good time."

When Cerise returned to her chamber late that morning, Thérèse was waiting for her, a sealed letter in her hands.

"It is from Sauveterre, chérie. Do you want me to open it?"

Cerise briefly closed her eyes, suddenly sure what was inside. She didn't want to see. Didn't want to know. But she must. There was no escaping it.

She opened the letter, read it, and then told Thérèse to lay out her black dress.

Then she closed the letter again, set it in the middle of her dressing table, and stared at the writing on the outside. Yes, it was meant for her. There was no mistake. Papa was dead.

Papa was dead, and she had failed him.

She pillowed her head on her arms and wept.

Cerise donned mourning black for her father and, along with the rest of the court, for the little Dauphin, seven-year-old Louis Joseph, the king's eldest son and heir. She had taken to walking in the garden apart from the other ladies, wanting to be alone with her thoughts and away from their chatter, with only Thérèse watching over her. From time to time, though Thérèse told her how ill-advised it was, Alexis Dieudonné would walk beside her, careful not to be seen.

"France has lost her next king, and it seems no one outside of Versailles has noticed," she said, feeling the queen's grief magnified by her own.

"Unless things change, France may find herself with no king at all."

She glanced back at Thérèse still a good distance behind them and then looked up at Alexis. "Hush. I will not hear treason against the king and queen."

He shook his head. "Do not misunderstand me. I have no ill will toward our sovereigns, but the mood of the people is ugly, dangerous. There are many who speak for freedom and equality without violence. But there are more who do not care whose blood is spilled as long as they have vengeance for centuries of wrongs."

"Please, monsieur, let us not speak of these matters. What can be done?"

"Forgive me," he said, his eyes full of sympathy. "I know your grief is deep."

"I promised Papa I would save Sauveterre, but"—she blinked back tears—"I was too slow. I was hoping he would at least know that Romain and I were betrothed."

Alexis snorted. "I beg your pardon, mademoiselle, but Monsieur le Vicomte is far more interested in his dice and his filles de joie than in being tied to a wife."

Her face reddened. "You should not speak of such things. For my father's sake, I will marry him, and so my son will be Vicomte de Guérin and of Proulx. Whatever else comes of it is in the hands of le bon Dieu."

He laughed softly. "And you think He would wish you to marry a man who does not love you and would not be faithful to you?"

She tossed her head, eyes flashing, and quickened her pace, leaving him behind. He was quick to catch up.

"Do not be angry. I merely speak as your friend."

"I have allowed you too much insolence, monsieur, in truth. But tell me, *my friend*, where I am to find such a man as you speak of. None of them at court is any different from Romain as far as I can tell."

"Perhaps you do not know where to look."

She huffed. "And you would know where?"

She strode forward still, not waiting for his response, not even looking to see how far back Thérèse was. Were all men idiots? They made the laws of society and then claimed to be baffled by the lengths women went to live under them.

"Mademoiselle."

She stopped abruptly, forcing him to stop too. "Well?"

There was a hint of mischief in his eyes. "I would tell you, truly, but it would only make you laugh."

That won at least a little bit of a smile from her. "Perhaps I would thank you for such a laugh right now."

He looked at her for a long while, and then he drew a deep breath. "I know that I—"

"Do you intend to spend the afternoon gossiping in the road?" Thérèse asked as she bustled past. "Come now, chérie, or you will not have time to dress for dinner."

"Wait," Alexis said softly, taking hold of Cerise's hand when she turned to follow. "Just for a moment, I beg you."

Cerise bit her lip, trying to read what was behind the urgent look in his eyes.

"Go on ahead, Thérèse," she called. "I will be right there."

Thérèse merely lifted one eyebrow and walked on.

Cerise turned to Alexis again and made her own voice low. "What is it?"

"You asked where at court you were to find a husband who would love you and be faithful to you. Shall I tell you?" He shook his head, a touch of wryness in his expression. "Here is where you would laugh at me, mademoiselle, but I know of no way but to say it." He put one hand over his heart. "I would be such a man."

"Alexis." Instead of the laughter he had predicted, tears swelled in her throat and filled her eyes. "You are—"

"I know. I am impertinent. I am a commoner. A servant."

She shook her head and forced a smile. "You are very sweet— and quite out of your mind."

"I am," he assured her, "but I am in earnest as well."

That urgency was again in his eyes, but there was a calm certainty there too. Surely it was the calm certainty of a madman.

"It is a fool's offer," she said, trying to sound scornful when in her heart of hearts she wanted to throw herself into his arms and be a fool too. "You know Sauveterre belongs to Romain now. My father left me nothing."

He shrugged. "Then we are equal in that. I also had such a father."

Now she did laugh, but it was a laugh of almost-hysterical hopelessness. "How would we live?"

"Would it not be my duty to provide for my own wife?"

She wanted to weep for the sweet, impractical simplicity of his answer. Instead she nodded. "Yes, of course. And after the great scandal and you are dismissed from the comte's service and I from court, what then? How will you provide for us?"

There was a glimmer of fervor in his dark eyes as if he only now dared speak a dream he had long held dear. "You have seen how my master looks to me to keep him at the vanguard of fashion. Could I not do so for others of the nobility, for my own profit, bound to no master? And you are such a wonder with your needle that you have caught the eye of the Queen of France herself. Would you not be sought after to adorn their ladies? Should we not make a fine pair, eh, you and I?"

She couldn't help an incredulous giggle. "I? A seamstress? A tailor's wife?"

The eagerness in his face died.

"And so you see, mademoiselle, I have indeed made you laugh."

She started to reach out to him, but then she drew her hand back, clasping it with the other in front of herself. She had hurt him, she knew, but it would be crueler to allow him to think such a plan would ever work.

"Monsieur," she began, "I did not intend—"

"No, no." He managed a smile and an airy wave of his hand. "I have offended you, and for that I apologize. I merely wished you to know you could make other choices, ones that do not include marrying a man you despise."

"Monsieur—"

"And perhaps," he said, an edge now to his tone, "those that do include marrying a man you love."

12

Cabot Falls, Vermont
Present Day

*W*hile she was making croissants as a bribe for her sisters, Sofia decided it might make things at the next play rehearsal a little less tense if she brought everyone a treat. Naomi had made some rather strident, if sugarcoated, general accusations at the last meeting that had done nothing to improve the unity of the group. Treats would surely help.

Later that afternoon, Sofia carried the tray to the auditorium, her purse and her bag of painting supplies slung over her shoulder. She was wondering how she was going to open the door when Davy and three of the other boys came racing down the hall toward her. All four of them skidded to a stop.

"Hi, Mrs. Parker," Davy said. "Do you need some help?"

"Thanks, Davy. Could you open the door for me?" She gave him a smile and nodded at the tray. "It'll be worth your while."

"Sure!" Davy held open one door and Connor held open the other.

"Hey, Brad, Jason," she addressed the other boys, "would you two clear off the table so I can set this down?"

She nodded toward the table set up in the corner, which was currently covered with various props and a stack of scripts. The boys, cooperative for once, dashed across the auditorium and moved everything onto the end of the stage just in time for Sofia to set down the tray. The obvious presence of treats drew a crowd.

"What is it?" Megan asked. "Is it for us?" Her hopeful smile was mirrored on three dozen other young faces.

Sofia grinned back. "This is an experiment. And you're all guinea pigs."

Connor frowned. "Guinea pigs?"

Still grinning, Sofia lifted the cover from the tray. There was a chorus of delighted *oohs* and *aahs* from the kids.

"What are those?" Heather asked, her freckled face beaming. "Did you make them?"

"Those," Sofia told her, "are called *palmiers*. Some people call them elephant ears or palm leaves. And yes, I made them. I thought you all would like to try them and let me know what you think."

"I don't like those," Connor said. "What do they taste like?"

Sofia forced herself not to laugh. "They're a pastry made with butter and sugar. If you like cookies, you'll probably like these."

"Well," he said thoughtfully, "maybe I could try one."

"Wait a minute, Connor!"

Sofia struggled to keep her exasperation from showing on her face as she turned. "Naomi. You're just in time. I thought we all deserved a little treat, and I wanted to try out this recipe, so—"

"That really was thoughtful of you, wasn't it, kids?" Naomi smiled thinly. "But I'm afraid you're going to have to put it all away. We don't have snacks at rehearsals. It's a matter of not having permission from all the parents and not knowing about allergies and such. And, of course, we don't need thirty-seven kids hopped up on sugar when we're trying to rehearse, do we? I'm sure you understand."

"But surely—"

"Now, now," Naomi said, her voice determinedly cheerful. "Rules are rules."

The kids groaned and went back to their scripts.

Sofia put the cover on the palmiers, but that didn't cover the tantalizing smell.

"Those do look delicious," Naomi said, "but really, you should check before springing something like this on me."

Sofia pressed her lips together briefly and then smiled. "Yes, I should have. I'll be sure to do that next time." *Your Majesty.*

Sofia plopped the tray of palmiers onto the kitchen counter. At least with her sisters and their families in town, four dozen elephant ears wouldn't go to waste. As she was rummaging through the refrigerator, trying to decide whether or not she needed to go to the grocery store, the back door banged open accompanied by a cold blast of air.

"Mom!" Vanessa and her friend Lindy bustled inside.

"I'm right here," Sofia said. "No need to shout. Hello, Lindy. How are you today?"

"Fine, Mrs. Parker, thanks."

"Lindy and I are going caroling with the youth group later," Vanessa said as she grabbed two elephant ears and offered one to her friend. "But first we're going to trade shoes."

Sofia's eyebrows went up. "Trade shoes?"

"Yeah, we wear the same size. So she brought a bunch of hers she hates, and she's going to see if any of the ones I hate are better."

Lindy was much taller than Vanessa, but she had a lean, runner's body and small feet.

"Suit yourselves," Sofia told them with a shake of her head. "If you end up with no shoes, that's on you."

Vanessa snickered.

"Ooh, these are great, Mrs. Parker," Lindy said around her second elephant ear. "I wish my mom would make these."

"Mom makes all kinds of good stuff," Vanessa bragged. "She's going to have her own bakery someday."

"Maybe," Sofia reminded her. "Someday."

"Do you make these to sell?" Lindy asked. "My dad's having some kind of thing at his office, and he was asking my mom what he should serve. I should tell him about these."

Sofia grinned. Sure, she had her hands full right now with the play and Christmas and guests from out of town. But when did she have spare time anyway? She'd never really have her own business if she didn't start sometime.

"You know," she said with a wink at Vanessa, "it really depends on what your dad is looking for. I make a lot of different kinds of things, but I'd love to talk to him about it." She jotted her name and cell phone number on the pad stuck to the refrigerator door and then tore off the page and handed it to Lindy. "Tell him he's welcome to call me if he's interested."

Lindy nodded. "Okay."

"Come on," Vanessa said, grabbing two more elephant ears to take with them, and they scurried out of the kitchen and up to her room.

"Well," Sofia said to herself as she returned to rummaging in the refrigerator, "talk about making lemons out of lemonade. Maybe I'll have my own bakery someday after all."

Sofia was a little late getting herself and Luke to rehearsal the next day. As quietly as possible, they hurried backstage. Luke started working on some of the props he and Jim had discussed the night before, and Sofia unpacked her paints and brushes. When she went out into the hall to get some water from the fountain for her brush well, she noticed Jason and Connor slipping in through the back door, both of them red-faced and furtive. They froze when they saw her.

"Mrs. Parker." Connor swallowed hard, dark eyes round.

Jason shifted on his feet, giving her a tentative, gap-toothed grin. "It's sure cold out."

Sofia put one finger to her lips, a reminder that rehearsal was going on. "What are you boys doing out without your coats?"

"We, uh"—Jason glanced at Connor—"we went to get some fresh air."

"I see." Sofia sniffed discreetly and was glad she didn't smell cigarette smoke. "I don't guess either of you knows anything about the shenanigans that have been going on around here, do you?"

Both boys shook their heads, all innocence.

"Because whoever's behind it is going to be in some pretty big trouble when he gets caught. He'd be smart to quit now, don't you think?"

"It's not us!" Connor protested.

"You two." Mr. Trumbull was standing in the door of one of the classrooms, a scowl on his weathered face. "I won't have you kids messing around out there. You got no business, hear me?"

The boys nodded and took off.

"Mr. Trumbull—" Sofia began.

"You neither, ma'am. I don't need to be cleaning up after any of you or pulling you out of trouble if you go where you don't belong."

Just then, Jim poked his head into the hall and gave her a wave. She felt more relieved to see him than she really ought to have.

He walked toward them. "How are you, Mr. Trumbull?"

The old man huffed. "Busier than I ought to be with all this going on."

"We appreciate you putting up with us," Jim said. "Before long, we'll all be out of your way. I'm sure Santa will have you on his nice list for being so patient."

Mr. Trumbull huffed again and shuffled away.

Jim put his arm around Sofia's shoulders and gave her a squeeze. "Everything okay?"

"Better now you're here," she said, keeping her voice low. "I'll tell you about it later."

"All right."

Onstage John, Michael, and Wendy were getting ready for bed. Sofia couldn't keep back a little grin when she saw Peter Pan slip behind the backdrop to watch Jim and Luke rigging more wires. It was a fairly simple system, but it would fill the bill nicely.

"What's this part called?" Kenny whispered, mindful of the rehearsal going on out front.

"Block and tackle," Jim replied, voice low. "That's what will take you up off the stage. This arm here is what moves you from side to side."

Kenny tilted his head. "Won't all the wires get tangled up? I mean with me and Megan and Wayne and Andy flying all at the same time?"

"Nah," Luke told him. "Dad's got it all worked out."

Jim nodded. "The other kids will only be able to fly up and down, and they'll be toward the back of the stage. You'll be the only one who can go up and down and side to side. And you'll be more toward the front of the stage. Their wires will be under and behind yours so nobody gets tangled."

Kenny grinned. "That's so cool."

"Kenny!"

Sofia cringed. None of them had noticed the dead silence onstage.

"Kenny!" Naomi stalked up the stage steps and back to where her truant son was standing. "That was your cue. Weren't you listening?"

Kenny shrugged, squirming. "I meant to. I was about to—"

"Come on." Naomi took her son's hand. "I don't have time to be tracking you down every time you're supposed to make an entrance. And Mr. Parker doesn't have time for your questions every five minutes." She gave Jim a rather stiff smile. "Sorry about that."

Before Jim could reply, she marched Kenny to the side of the stage where he'd make his entrance.

"All right, Megan," she called as she clattered back down the steps and out into the house. "Give us Kenny's cue again."

Mouth taut, Sofia looked at Jim, but he only put one finger to his lips as the rehearsal continued. She knew it was more than a reminder to keep her voice down. With a huff, she went back to painting the night sky over London, black and midnight blue awash with stars. Gleaming in the silver light far in the distance were the Thames, St. Paul's Cathedral, Tower Bridge, and the Tower itself. Tension flowed out of her as she painted, and by the time rehearsal was over and the night backdrop was finished, she had decided what to do.

Most of the kids had already gone, whisked away by busy parents. Davy and Jason and Connor were playing some variety of tag up and down the stage, in the corridor, and who knew where else, no doubt waiting to be picked up by one parent or the other. Luke and Jim were carrying tools out to the car, and Kenny was sitting in the front row of the audience, kicking his heels against the seat as he waited for his mother to finish with her notes for tomorrow's rehearsal.

Sofia smiled at her. "I know it's got to be a handful, trying to keep everything moving in the right direction with kids this age."

Naomi shrugged, still writing. "Just have to stay organized."

"True. True. They get distracted so easily." Sofia laughed softly. "But sometimes you have to let them pursue what interests them."

Naomi looked at her, one eyebrow slightly lifted, waiting for her to go on.

"I just . . . well, Kenny seems really interested in the set building and other technical parts of the show. I was wondering if he might not like it better helping out backstage. You know, Jim would be happy to teach him about tools and building things."

"Sofia, I appreciate all of your hard work with the sets." Naomi clutched her clipboard against her chest. "You and Jim are doing a great job, and I haven't interfered with whatever you've decided to do as far as that's concerned. But for all the rest, especially as far as my own son is concerned, I really have to see to that myself. Don't you agree?" She managed a not-too-convincing smile.

Sofia nodded. "Of course. I didn't mean to suggest anything else. I thought Kenny might be happier . . ."

Davy and the other two boys breezed past them, jostling one another.

"Don't be late tomorrow," Naomi called after them. "Not too many more rehearsals left."

"I know," Davy said, and they scurried out the door.

"Anyway," Sofia continued, "I was wondering if Kenny was really happy being—"

"Are you trying to get him to give up the lead? Is that what this is about?"

Sofia blinked. "No. It's not about that. I only—"

"Maybe your son would be better in the role? Is that it?"

Sofia couldn't help an incredulous laugh. "No, not at all. Luke isn't interested in acting. I'm not even sure he's actually interested in theater. Mostly he wants to work with his dad. But this is about Kenny, not Luke. He's seemed so unhappy—"

Naomi's eyes flashed. "Kenny is a quiet boy, but that doesn't mean he's not happy."

"I just thought you might want to talk to him about it."

"Fine. Kenny?"

Sofia cringed. "I didn't mean right now."

Naomi strode over to where Kenny was sitting, and Sofia couldn't do anything but follow her.

Kenny looked up at his mother and then at Sofia and then back at his mother, clearly wishing he were somewhere else. "Yeah, Mom?"

"I want you to tell me something."

Again, Kenny glanced at Sofia. "What?"

"Tell me the real truth now," Naomi said. "I won't be mad."

He frowned. "Tell you what?"

"Do you really want to be Peter Pan? Or would you rather let your understudy take over the role?"

There was a little flicker in the boy's eyes. "I guess Davy *is* better than I am. I'd understand if you'd rather let him do it. I want the play to be good and everything."

Naomi looked at Sofia. "He never gives himself enough credit for what he's good at." She turned again to her son. "No, I think you're the best one for the part. But that's not what I'm asking here. I'm only trying to make sure you *want* to do it. We'll be doing the play in a very short while, of course, but that's all right. It's never easy to change the lead this far into rehearsals, but we can do it. I want you to tell me what you really think. If you want to let the backup step in on opening night, that's okay."

Sofia bit her lip. *Great way to set the kid up, Naomi.*

Kenny opened his mouth, then ducked his head and sank down a little in his seat. "It's kind of late to change now, right?"

"I don't want anyone thinking I made you do it when you didn't want to."

He shook his head, not looking at her.

"Sometimes," Naomi added, "it seems like you want to be working backstage instead of acting."

"You know, Kenny, Luke's dad doesn't mind showing you things with the tools and all that," Sofia said.

Kenny shrugged. "That's all right, Mrs. Parker. I guess I really should just do my lines and stuff and not bother him. Thanks anyway."

"You're welcome, Mrs. Parker," Naomi said, a touch of smugness in her expression. "I guess we're done for tonight. Ready to go?"

"Ready." He stood up. "See you later, Mrs. Parker."

Sofia smiled at him. "Sure thing, Kenny. Tomorrow."

He and his mother walked toward the door. Then Kenny stopped. "Forgot my backpack."

He dashed up the stage steps and behind the set, his feet clattering on the boards and then on the linoleum. A moment later, he was back, the pack over his shoulder.

"Bye!" He darted out the door with Naomi.

Sofia stood for a moment, staring at the door, knowing her face was flushed. *Poor Kenny. How could anyone be so blind? Especially a mother.*

"You the last one?"

She turned, startled to see Mr. Trumbull coming up the aisle with his push broom.

"I guess I am," she said brightly. "I hope you don't have much more to do before you get to go home."

He frowned. "Sweep up. Lock up. That's about it."

"Well, have a good night." She picked up her purse and her bag of supplies.

The door swung open, and Luke popped his head inside. "You get lost or something, Mom?"

She exhaled heavily and smiled. "Coming."

13

Palace of Versailles, France
June 1789

*C*erise's face turned hot. She was glad they were in a part of the palace garden where they would not be observed. "I love no one, monsieur."

"No one, mademoiselle?" Alexis's dark eyes gleamed. "Do you not even allow for the possibility?"

She pursed her lips. "I think I would be the very first to know."

"Oh, you would know, and I think you *do* know."

She lifted one eyebrow. "You?"

He bowed slightly. The man was not only impertinent, he was insolent. He was outrageous!

She drew herself up as disdainfully as she could. "As I said, monsieur, I love no one."

"I do not believe that is so." His mouth turned up the slightest bit on one side, and his playful humor returned. "You merely haven't courage enough to confess it."

"Sometimes courage is only a pleasant name for foolhardiness," she said coolly. *How dare he call me a coward?*

"And sometimes prudence is only cowardice in disguise."

"I see. And do you think every lady at court is in love with you and afraid to admit it?"

"Oh no." His face was the picture of perfect innocence. "Only one."

With a sigh, she started walking again, and he followed

121

obediently behind her. How could she stay angry with him?

They soon reached the more open part of the garden, a place where she and Alexis could not be seen together.

Thérèse was standing there, hands on hips. "At last. I thought perhaps you had decided to set up a shop in there."

Cerise frowned at her but said nothing.

"Your pardon, madame," Alexis said. "You ought to go in now. We do not wish mademoiselle to be missed." There was a twinkle in his eye. "You know my master sometimes sends me out to follow you, to see where you go and whom you meet."

Cerise glared at him. "How dare he!"

"Do not let it trouble you. I can honestly report to him that I never see you walking out with anyone but your maid."

Thérèse chuckled, and Cerise couldn't suppress a smile.

"If only you were of noble blood," Cerise said. "Then you might have asked for my hand and protected me from such attentions."

He did not smile in return. "These are uncertain times. A man of high standing and great wealth might in the blink of an eye find himself without either."

She shook her head, her smile fading. "You and your rebel friends, you act as if all the world were coming down around our ears. We have always had a king and the nobility. It has always been better to be rich than poor. I will not throw myself into the gutter because you see revolution around every corner."

"You would rather throw yourself into misery with a man you do not love?"

A hot reply sprang to her tongue, but then she softened. "It may not seem wise to you. You are, as you rightly say, a man with nothing whose father had nothing. You have never known anything else. But I was raised with certain standards. Certain expectations. I . . ." She looked away from him, suddenly feeling very weak and contemptible. "I would not know how to live any other way."

Neither of them spoke for the longest while.

Then he touched her chin with one gentle finger, turning up her face so her gaze met his. "I could teach you."

She forced a light laugh. "I see you are impractical in love as well as in politics, monsieur. But, alas, I cannot afford such fancies. The pride of my family's name and place meant much to my father. I gave him my pledge that his grandson and that child's son and grandson would keep it for remembrance of him."

The softness left his eyes and his mouth tightened. "And suppose Monsieur le Vicomte Lévesque does not care to fulfill that wish of your father's? Then what?"

"He . . . he simply must."

For a moment he was silent, and then he exhaled heavily. "Forgive me. I did not mean to anger you. I merely hoped you might . . ." He smiled a little, softness once again in his eyes, but he said no more.

"Might what?"

He shrugged. "The world is changing. Faster than any of us ever thought it would. And we who live in it must change or die."

His words terrified her, though she refused to show it. How could she change? What could she be besides what she was? If his fears proved true, what would become of her?

Before she could reply, she heard someone calling for her. With a swift bow, Alexis hurried off in the opposite direction.

Cerise stepped out from the concealment of the trees with Thérèse behind her.

Catching sight of her, Romain smiled. "Good day to you, mademoiselle!"

Cerise gathered up her black skirts and made a deep curtsy. "Monsieur le Vicomte. You seem very well today."

Romain was dressed in peach satin, and his powdered wig sported a ribbon to match. As always, his blue eyes sparkled with mischief and good humor. "Alas, mon chou, I am desolate, simply desolate."

She tried to be sympathetic, but it was difficult to pity someone who so clearly was not grieving. "What is it?"

"Will you believe it? Mademoiselle Plamondon, the little minx, says she will not have me."

Cerise blinked, not certain she had heard him properly. Then hope flooded through her once again. *Oh, Papa, perhaps I have not failed you after all.*

She attempted a look of concern, though she was certain she failed miserably. "She has refused you? But has not Her Majesty said—"

"Oh, indeed. But she will not marry so foolish a popinjay as Monsieur le Vicomte de Guérin." Romain laughed heartily. "I swear, my pretty cousin, I think I must have her now, freckles and squints and all. Sacré bleu! What a fierce little savage she must be. I shall put on my very most fetching manner and woo her, shall I not?"

"But if it is something her mother and the queen wish, why should she refuse?"

He looked quickly around the garden and then leaned closer to her, lowering his voice. "Someone, it seems, told her that besides being a frivolous ne'er-do-well, I was rather overfond of the tavern." He grinned. "But whether it is the drink or the filles de joie of which she does not approve, well, she did not deign to say. Which do you think, petite?"

Cerise's cheeks burned, and she did not look at him. Surely Thérèse was scowling now. If things went as Cerise hoped, she had better learn to overlook such matters. She had better not think of where he had been and with whom. Her sons would be his heirs. Sauveterre would stay in her family. Knowing of his escapades was no greater a humiliation than most noblemen's wives suffered. Could she truly expect anything better?

"But will she not change her mind?"

"That is what I so admire. She says she would rather go to the convent than give herself to a libertine. How can I not admire her?"

Cerise could not help admiring the girl herself. Oh, to have such courage. To say she would do as the leading of her heart, her conscience, and le bon Dieu told her and nothing more? *What blessed freedom.*

But she knew she did not herself possess such courage. At the least, Romain seemed a good-natured man. She never felt frightened in his presence. She never felt as if she were being lured into a cage. And if he were not likely to keep his marriage vows, she supposed there was little she could do about that. Was there any man at court, excepting the good king himself, who kept faith with his wife?

Of its own accord, there flashed into her mind the image of Alexis standing with his hand over his heart, his velvet eyes concealing nothing. *I would be such a man.*

"My cousin?"

She blinked her stinging eyes and smiled up at Romain. "Monsieur?"

"Do you wish to continue our little pleasantries about Sauveterre now that your dear papa has gone to his reward?"

She gave him a coquettish pout, knowing tears would only repel him. "You tease me again. Even at the height of my mourning, still you tease."

He put her arm through his and patted her hand. "We cannot always mourn. What will be is what will be and cannot be changed. But we can think on what is pleasant. And I am of the mind that it would be most pleasant to join the game of faro there on the other side of the fountain."

They began to walk that way.

"Your maman ought to be told at once," Cerise said.

"There is time and plenty for such grave matters."

"We are made no guarantees. Any of us might die in the next moment."

He gave her his habitual cheeky grin. "Anyone, mon chou, save myself."

That surprised her into a laugh. "And you are certain of this?"

"Oh, quite. Quite. My good papa put by a bottle of the finest brandy on the day I was born. Before he died, he told me I should keep it and open it to celebrate the greatest day of my life. So, you see, I have not yet had that day, and I have not yet opened that bottle. So, naturally, I cannot die." Again he patted her hand. "Now, shall we try our fortune at faro?"

And thinking that she might do as Papa had wished after all, she could not help smiling.

Three days later, Romain came to Cerise as she sat sewing in the garden.

"My little cousin," he said with a deep bow, "it seems news travels swiftly in our modern days. I have had a letter from Maman." He waved a densely filled piece of paper before her. "It seems that before his death, your papa wrote to my uncle, the Duc de Deschamps, about our little . . . situation. The duc has told Maman that it is time I made at least a pretense of taking my position seriously."

She looked up from the piece of silk she was beading for the queen's new gown.

He plopped himself down on the marble bench beside her, looking as if he had just been sentenced to death. "When my papa died, he made my uncle trustee of all my inheritance until I should marry or reach the age of twenty-five. Until that time, I live upon his charity."

"And Uncle has given you an ultimatum."

He dropped his head into his hands with a heavy sigh. "Either I find a wife or I beg my bread for the next three years."

She pulled her eyes back to her work, not wanting him to see the freshly kindled hope in them. *Oh, Papa, perhaps now. Perhaps now.*

She gave him the mildest of questioning glances. "And why do you come to me?"

He looked up, and she had to force herself not to laugh at the genuine tragedy in his expression. "Ah, now it is you who toys with me. I have Sauveterre, and your father wished your children also to have it. So. Shall we agree together and then perhaps have my uncle speak to the queen of it?"

She lowered her eyes modestly. "Surely, monsieur, there are ladies more gracious, more worthy, more—"

He slapped his hands on his thighs and then bounced to his feet. "Must we play at this? Come, little cousin, we understand each other, do we not? Let us make a bargain and be done with this foolishness. I am to play cards with the Vicomte de Linville at three, and I do not like to be late."

She blinked at him. After all this time, he was finally agreeing to what she had asked and on the terms she had originally offered, but now . . .

"Oh, do agree. We get on well enough, do you not think so? What more do you wish?"

She drew a deep breath and then nodded rapidly. "Nothing more. If your uncle will speak to the queen of it, then we shall be agreed."

"Excellent. Excellent." He seized her hand and brushed his lips against her knuckles. "I will see to it at once. After my game, of course. I trust you will not insist we marry soon."

She motioned to her somber skirts. "I am in mourning, as you well know, and will be until Noel at the least."

He caught up her hand, this time pressing it with a fervent kiss. "It is good of you. Very good of you."

A moment later he was striding back toward the palace, and

she watched him until she could see him no more. Well, it was done at last. *Be happy, Papa. Sauveterre will go to your grandson and to those who follow him.* She wondered how much he would lose today to the vicomte, how much his gambling had cost him already, how much it would cost him as the years rolled along. Well, here at Versailles, it seemed it was considered poor taste not to be in debt. Her husband-to-be was certainly stylish in that respect.

She closed her eyes, her needle still for once. She clutched it tightly between her fingers. This was what she had wished. There were worse things, she knew, than being tied forever to a man with the vanity and the intelligence of a peacock. It was done.

For a few more minutes, she attempted to work on her beading, but it was no use. She could not concentrate. If she were not more careful, she would ruin the piece entirely. She rubbed her weary eyes, gathered her things, and set off toward the palace. But as she walked, she realized someone was behind her.

Alexis.

14

Palace of Versailles, France
June 1789

$\mathcal{C}$erise turned pale. Had Alexis overheard her conversation with Romain? Bah, he was a servant. A valet. What was the opinion of such a man to her? She would not even notice him.

But as she stepped through the doorway back into the palace, she heard his low whisper. "Mademoiselle Bélanger."

She stopped where she was and then moved a little way down the corridor.

"Mademoiselle?"

Glancing around to see she was not being observed, she turned around. It would not do to have him speaking to her unless it was concerning some business of his master's.

He made a deep bow. "Pardon my forwardness, but I must speak to you."

"You have a message from the comte?" she asked, her expression cool.

"I do, and it would be wise for anyone who may pass by to think that is all we speak of."

Her cheeks grew warmer, but she did not change her expression. "And what more could there possibly be?"

He pressed his lips together, obviously stung. "Nothing, mademoiselle. I humbly crave your pardon. My master the comte asks if he might call for you this afternoon to go riding in his carriage. I shall bring to him your regrets."

He bowed again and turned to go. No, he could not go. Not quite yet. Not until she could explain.

"Monsieur Dieudonné." She sighed. "Alexis."

He stopped where he was. For the longest time, he did not move. Then he turned once more to her, as impersonal as any servant.

"Mademoiselle?"

"You . . . you must have heard. Vicomte Lévesque, I mean." Her eyes pleaded with him for pity, for understanding, for she did not know what. "You must know—"

"My master sent me to you, and I meant to wait until you were no longer occupied. I did not overhear your conversation except for a few words. But I see the assumptions I made were not unwarranted." His expression softened into sorrow. "So you will give yourself to this witless fop?"

She dropped her head, ashamed now to look into those velvet eyes, knowing they reflected the disappointment and doubt coming from her own heart.

"I must," she said. "You know I must. For Papa's sake. For Sauveterre." Tears pooled in her eyes. She had to clasp her hands together to keep them from reaching toward him. "Please, monsieur. Alexis. Do not think too harshly of me."

"Oh, chérie." He looked as if he were bleeding inwardly.

She managed a pleading mockery of a smile. "Vicomte Lévesque, he is not so terrible a fellow, is he? And he is not witless. He is merely careless and rather frivolous. He is hardly more than a boy yet, and boys one day grow up. You will see."

Now the sorrow in his expression was mixed with pain and pleading. "Do not agree to this, I beg you. You cannot. You must not. In your very heart, you know it is the wrong thing for you."

A tear slipped down her cheek, but she batted it away, not wanting him to see. "It will not be for some months yet.

Vicomte Lévesque understands I will be in mourning almost until Noel."

"But Noel will come, mademoiselle. It will come."

"Alexis"—she clasped her hands more tightly together, certain they were going to betray her—"do not abandon me now."

"Abandon you?" The words were barely audible, half-choked. "No." He shook his head slightly and said nothing more. He made another deep bow, his features again perfectly schooled. "I will convey your regrets to my master."

Once again, he turned to go. Once again, she called him back. "Mademoiselle?"

"Please understand. It is what must be."

His impersonal expression did not change, but there was something darker now behind his eyes. "It is many months until Noel. By then, perhaps God will send an angel to deliver you from such a travesty."

With that, he bowed and disappeared down the corridor.

Alexis came to her the next morning as she again sat in the garden with her beadwork. "Mademoiselle." He bowed and handed her a message. "From my master. Felicitations upon your coming betrothal."

Her eyes widened. "He knows already? I thought he was in Paris."

"He is, but by now all the world knows. Vicomte Lévesque told the Duc de Deschamps, his uncle, and . . . May I take the comte any reply?"

She looked down at the message and shook her head. He was still there when she looked up a moment later. "Monsieur?"

He ducked his head. When he finally spoke, his voice was very low and swift. "I have come to beg your pardon. When we last spoke, I was angry. I was too angry. I know that you of the nobility have a duty to your ancestors and to the honorable names you bear. It is not right for me to ask you to abandon all that when I can give you nothing in return."

Nothing but his tender heart.

"But know, ma chère mademoiselle," he continued, "that I have spoken truly. Circumstances may part us, but you will forever have my love."

She swallowed down the emotion that swelled in her throat. Oh, to be able to throw herself into his arms and not care who might see! To even take hold of his hand and cling to it as they talked. But she could only give him a grateful and not-too-noticeable smile that passersby would think nothing of.

"Can we not have things as they were?" she said. "We need change nothing, at least not until I am married. Talk to me and be my friend. Let us have this time for us before we need let it go."

"And after?"

She could only shrug and give him what she hoped was a brave smile. "After? Well, we will leave after in the hands of Providence. It may be that we concern ourselves now over nothing. From this time to that, things may well change."

And he smiled too.

The Comte de Therin-Toussant returned from Paris that very afternoon. "Well well, I see things have fallen out as you have wished." He bowed over Cerise's hand. "You are to be much congratulated."

She curtsied. "I thank you, monsieur."

He tucked her arm through his and started them walking. "Chérie, I am gone to Paris a day and a night, and see what we have. What other mischief have you been at while I was away?"

"It has been very quiet. I have done my sewing, but little else. We hear tales from Paris and even in the countryside of the people wishing to rule themselves. Is it so?"

"Bah, the people do not know what they want. Every breeze turns them. And these firebrands who set them off with their tales, His Majesty would do well to have them rounded up and sent to the scaffold. But why do we waste our breath on such animals when we might have so many more pleasant things to discuss?"

True to their agreement, Romain made no objections to her carriage rides with the comte. But these days, the comte was in and out of the palace, sometimes to Paris, sometimes to his own estate. Sometimes he sent Alexis to see to his affairs, usually only to Paris, sometimes to various places nearby. But today he had gone himself and left Alexis behind.

Cerise felt as though it were a holiday, and she wanted to enjoy herself. Perhaps if it were carefully planned, she might steal a moment or two to speak with Alexis. Before she knew it, it would be Noel and she would be married to Romain. Then these little trysts, innocent as they were, would have to stop.

She saw him in the garden, cutting roses, and smiled to think, though it was by the comte's orders, that the flowers she received every day came from Alexis. She peered around the corner, making sure the two of them were quite alone. Then she crept up behind him, her velvet slippers soundless on the path.

He was kneeling now, and it was easy to lean down and cover his eyes with her hands.

"Guess—"

He threw her off with a gasp, tossing the roses to the ground and brandishing the long shears like a weapon, his eyes wild. Then that wildness died. He used his coat sleeve to blot the sudden sweat from his upper lip.

"I beg your pardon, mademoiselle." He bowed, eyes still wary. "I was not expecting anyone."

She gave him a tentative smile, seeing one of the thorns had bloodied his hand. "No, it is I who should apologize. I meant only to tease you. I did not mean to frighten you."

"You merely startled me." He dabbed at the blood with his handkerchief and then stuffed it back into his coat pocket. "I had thought I was quite alone."

"That is why I came to see you. Where have you been all day?"

He knelt again and gathered the discarded flowers, not meeting her gaze. "I have been attending to matters for my master. I have time for very little else."

She lifted one eyebrow. "I see. Then I shall not trouble you either."

She swept her skirts to one side and turned to go back the way she came. But she paused, waiting for him to stop her.

"Mademoiselle?"

At last. She smiled to herself. She would forgive him, of course, if he were abject enough. She would forgive him. Then they would talk, and she would feel as if Noel were years and years away from now. She waited a moment longer and turned to him, her expression cool and imperious. "Yes?"

For one brief second, she saw despair in his dark eyes, eyes that pled for her not to leave him there alone. Then every trace of emotion was gone. He was only a servant, impersonal and without feelings.

"Good afternoon, mademoiselle." With a bow, he turned back to the roses and knelt again.

She watched him for a moment, and then she came up beside him. "Monsieur?"

Finally he glanced back at her, and then he got to his feet. "Forgive me. I am not myself this afternoon." He blinked and looked away again.

"Please, monsieur, what is it?"

He peered over her shoulder and back toward the palace. Then he finally faced her, that wildness again in his eyes.

"Take care. These are dangerous times. One can never be certain who is to be trusted."

"What has happened?"

"Nothing." There was a hint of a bitter smile on his lips. "Nothing that can be remedied now."

Her heart beat a little faster, a little more unsteadily. "You frighten me."

"You should be frightened. Indeed, you should."

With a curt bow, he hurried away, the roses clutched in his arms.

15

Cabot Falls, Vermont
Present Day

Sofia carried two cups of tea into their bedroom, handed one to Jim, and curled up on the bed next to him with a sigh, glad for the late-night quiet and the knowledge there was no rehearsal the next day and all of their company was settled for the night.

He put down his book and put one arm around her. "What is it? And don't tell me nothing."

She wrinkled her nose at him. "Smarty."

He chuckled. "So? Tell me."

She shook her head. "Oh, I don't know. Nothing. Everything."

She told him what had happened that afternoon with Jason and Connor and Mr. Trumbull.

"I can't help thinking those boys are up to something, but I haven't been able to figure out what it is. And Mr. Trumbull isn't going to be happy until all of us leave him and his auditorium alone."

"But you don't have any hard evidence against anyone," Jim said. "We'll have to keep our eyes open. Whoever our vandal is, he's got to give himself away eventually."

"I wish I hadn't gotten mixed up in this stupid play in the first place."

Surprised to feel tears stinging her eyes, she gave him a sheepish smile. He squeezed her a little closer to him.

"Naomi again?"

"Always." She exhaled heavily. "I know you told me to stay out of it. I know I should have."

"Did you two have another run-in?"

She nodded. "While you and Luke were packing up the car."

He chuckled. "We couldn't have been out there five minutes."

"I know. Brilliant me, I thought maybe I could get her to talk to Kenny. It's so obvious that he doesn't want to be in the play, that he wants to help you backstage."

"And she wouldn't hear of it, eh?"

"No." She took a sip of coffee, letting the warmth soothe her from the inside out. "She did ask him, in front of me, of course, if he wanted to quit. He's too afraid of disappointing her to tell her the truth."

"Maybe it *is* the truth," he suggested.

She scoffed. "You don't believe that any more than I do."

"Well, it doesn't seem that way. But he is her son. I mean, we wouldn't much like it if she told us how to raise ours, would we?"

She frowned. "Yeah, I know."

"And it is kind of late to get a new Peter Pan at this point."

She shrugged. "I don't think so. Davy would do a good job, and he's definitely more excited about it than Kenny is. But Naomi wouldn't hear of it."

"And what about you?" he asked when she didn't say anything else. "It's kind of late to get a new set designer too, isn't it?"

She pursed her lips. "Oh, all right. I won't quit. I'll be extranice and extrapatient and finish up the job." She snuggled a little closer to him. "Just like you, though I don't know how you put up with her and never lose your temper."

He chuckled. "I simply go home every day glad nobody hears what I don't say."

"I know what you mean." She laid her head on his shoulder,

finally feeling the tension from that afternoon slip away. "I'll soldier on."

"Good." He turned his head a little, nuzzling his lips against her hair. "You know, it's not really much of a gift if it doesn't cost you anything. We're doing this for the kids and for the school, not for Naomi."

"True. And maybe we can make it a little easier on Kenny too." She considered for a minute. "I did have some good news today."

"Yes?"

"Lindy, Vanessa's friend, told her dad about my palmiers, and he called to ask me about the kinds of things I make. He ended up hiring me to cater his office Christmas party."

"Hey, that's great!" Jim gave her a smacking kiss.

"It'll help our fractured finances. Who knows? Maybe one of my talents will start paying off."

"You bet," he said, a softness coming into his expression. "I've always believed in your talents, you know."

She took his cup from him and set both of theirs down on the bedside table. Then she put her arms around his neck, smiling into his eyes. "Did I ever tell you I think you're a pretty nice guy?"

He chuckled, touching his nose to hers. "A time or two. Even when I didn't deserve it."

She nestled against him again, suddenly thinking of the girl from the diary and how glad she was to be married to the man she wanted, the one she loved, the one who loved her, her best friend. No matter the splendor of the Palace of Versailles, she was glad she was not Cerise Bélanger.

"Can I try that?"

Sofia looked up from her painting to see Kenny at Jim's side as he used his power drill.

Jim glanced toward the front of the stage. "Are you sure your mom won't mind?"

"We're on a break," Kenny said, looking that way too. "She went to make some copies of a new song for Megan and the lady that plays the piano. She said we could have fifteen minutes off. I won't be missing any cues or anything."

Jim grinned. "Sure. Give it a try."

He gave Kenny the drill and held it with him as he drove in a screw. Sofia smiled, watching the two of them. Jim was always such a patient dad, even with someone else's kids.

"That's good," he told the boy, "but the screw needs to go straight through the brace into the frame or it'll come apart. Let me show you."

He reversed the drill and twirled the screw back out of the wood.

"Hey, how'd you do that?" Kenny asked, tilting his head sideways.

"Just flip this lever right here," Jim explained, showing him. "This way is forward, and this way is backward. Now, let's try this one again."

He held the screw straight and, with a quick whir, drove it into the wood. He handed the next screw to Kenny.

"All right, put this one right there."

Kenny picked up the nail Jim had used before and hammered it about a third of the way in, right at the pencil mark Jim showed him. Then he pulled it out and set the screw in the hole he had made.

"Straight now," Jim said.

"Right." Kenny held the screw and fitted the drill bit into the end of it. He slowly squeezed the trigger, flinching a little as it growled and then whirred. This time the screw went in straight. The boy beamed at Jim. "I did it! It's right, isn't it?"

"I couldn't have done better." Jim clasped his shoulder and then pointed to the brace on the other side of the frame. "Want to take care of that side for me?"

"Sure!"

Jim carried his plans and tape measure to the middle of the frame and marked where the doorway would go. Kenny took the hammer and the nail, a handful of screws, and the drill to the other end of the frame. As Jim had showed him, he used the nail to make a pilot hole at every place that was marked. Then he fitted a screw into the first one.

"Uh, Mr. Parker? Do you want to come make sure I'm doing it right?"

"Nah, you're fine. Full speed ahead."

Grinning, Kenny squeezed the trigger. He flinched again as the drill started to buzz, but he held it steady. The screw went in straight and flush. With a glance at Jim, he picked up another screw, put it in place, and fitted the drill bit into the slot. Confident this time, he squeezed the trigger.

"Kenny!"

The drill roared and then ground to a stop. The screw was sticking out of the wood at an awkward angle.

"Mom." Kenny bit his lip and looked again at Jim. "I was, um . . ."

Naomi pursed her lips and gave Jim an apologetic smile. "I'm sorry. He knows better than to play with things that don't belong to him. Give Mr. Parker back his drill now, Kenny. Time to get back to rehearsal."

"Mom, I wasn't—"

"He wasn't playing," Jim said. "He was helping me. And doing a pretty good job of it too."

Naomi gave the wayward screw the briefest of glances and nodded. "Well, from now on I'll keep a better eye on him while you're working. Tell Mr. Parker you're sorry, Kenny."

Kenny hung his head. "Sorry, Mr. Parker."

"Nothing to be sorry for, Ken," Jim said, clasping his shoulder. "Thanks for giving me a hand."

"Come along now, Kenny," Naomi said in her no-nonsense voice.

Eyes on the floor, Kenny followed her to the front of the stage.

Sofia went over to Jim, blood boiling. "Ooh, she makes me so mad! I had to bite my tongue before I said something not suitable for little ears."

His mouth turned up a little on one side. "Can't say that didn't run through my mind too. Poor kid."

She nodded. "You have a devoted fan."

His smile turned a little sheepish. "We men have to stick together, you know?" He gave her shoulders a comforting squeeze. "Now come on. We both need to get back to work too."

She glanced toward the stage. How she'd like to give that woman a piece of her mind and then some.

Not my job. My job is to get this scenery painted, not to run other people's lives for them.

She dredged up a smile, gave Jim a kiss on the cheek, and went back to her work. As soon as she finished the backdrop for the Indian camp, she left it to dry and went back to put the final touches on the mermaid lagoon. When she lifted the canvas covering it, she gasped.

Someone had splashed black paint all over it.

Sofia managed to salvage the lagoon backdrop, but it took her most of the afternoon. Once again, nobody seemed to have seen anything or know anything about how it happened. She was still seething later that night as she cubed cooked chicken for a casserole. It wasn't the wanton destruction of her work that made her angriest. It was everything else, especially Naomi. That woman had humiliated her own son in front of Jim. At least it hadn't been in front of the other kids, though Naomi had done that often enough too. Opening night couldn't come soon enough.

After she dumped the chicken into a bowl, she picked up a bell pepper, plunged a paring knife into the top near the stem, and cut a jagged hole. Obviously Kenny needed a male role model, someone he could look up to, and Jim was a great choice. She removed the stem and wrenched the pepper in two with both hands. But there had to be someone in the boy's own family who could at least do something toward filling his absent father's place. An uncle or a grandfather or a cousin once or twice removed. Somebody.

She gave the pepper a quick rinse to wash out the seeds and returned it to the cutting board. Maybe Naomi couldn't help it that her husband was long gone, but she didn't have to smother and belittle her son because of it. The little knife thumped against the cutting board as Sofia made quick work of the pepper and then an onion, her hands deft and sure as she chopped them.

Dratted school play. Why did she have to get involved with it in the first place? What with Wynter's therapy, Christmas preparations, her new catering job, and the everyday chaos of keeping track of four kids plus her niece and nephew, she hadn't really needed more to do. And Naomi wasn't making her any happier about having volunteered.

Sofia dumped the chopped vegetables into the bowl with the cubed chicken and added the leftover green beans from last night. "The nerve of the woman," she muttered as she thrust a can of creamed corn under the opener and snapped down the lever. "I swear, one more thing and I'll—"

She started as the back door slammed shut.

Matthew ran across the kitchen floor with a huge grin, leaving a trail of muddy slush in his wake. "Hi, Mom!"

"Matthew!" She set the opened can on the countertop, sloshing creamed corn down the side. "What have I told you about slamming that door? And what have you been into? Look at your shoes! And look at my floor!"

"I'm sorry, Mom, I—"

"Why do you have to do this all the time?" She dumped the creamed corn into the bowl with the rest of the ingredients. Then she snatched up a section of the morning paper and spread it on the floor. "Put your shoes on that before you get mud anywhere else. Good heavens, Matthew, do you think I don't have enough to do already? Do you have to leave a mess wherever you go? What were you thinking?"

Blue eyes full of tears, he held out a scraggly handful of winterberries, hemlock boughs, and red maple twigs, a colorful red-and-green winter bouquet. "I only wanted to get these for you. They looked pretty, and I thought you'd like to have them so the table would look nice for company."

"Oh, Matthew." She knelt down and took him into her arms. "I'm sorry, honey. I'm so, so sorry."

She held him close to her, pressing her lips to his tangled hair. He had only wanted to do something nice for her, and she had unloaded all her own frustrations on his ten-year-old shoulders. Well, that had to stop. She was *not* going take Naomi home with her. Not ever again.

"Let me see," she said, smiling into her son's eyes as she pulled back from him and then looked at the bouquet. "Those *are* very pretty. You know, I don't think I've ever had wildflowers in the winter before." She didn't spoil it by telling him some of the plants were toxic.

He sniffled and gave her a crooked smile in return. "I saw them at the side of the road. I didn't mean to mess up the floor."

"It's just a floor, sweetie. Nothing I should lose my temper over. Forgive me?"

He nodded, his smile a little more convincing. "I'll clean it up."

She kissed his forehead and stood up, holding out her hand. "*We'll* clean it up."

16

Palace of Versailles, France
June 1789

For a long moment, Cerise stood there among the roses, staring after Alexis. She wrapped her arms around herself, feeling a sudden chill in the heat of the afternoon. She did not want to be here now. Not alone. Too many trees. Too many shadows.

She gathered her skirts and hurried back into the palace, past the guards and courtiers and servants, past the normal bustle of the court. By the time she reached her chamber, her heart had slowed to a more normal pace. She laughed at the reflection she saw in her glass, pink-cheeked, wide-eyed, and giddy as a goose.

"You *are* a goose." She gave herself her prettiest smile as she rearranged one tangled curl and straightened the lace at her neckline. "Monsieur Dieudonné worries too much about matters that should be left to the king and his ministers. Little wonder he is so unhappy."

She turned to look at herself from the back and then frowned. Her hair had come undone at the nape of her neck. Before Cerise could send for her, Thérèse came into the room, hands in the air and out of breath.

"Ma chéri, you have heard? And just this morning, before dawn. Heaven help us all in this wicked world! Barely outside the stable where he left his horse. Oh!" She clasped her hands and sat heavily on the chair by the window. "And of course the fool of a groom heard nothing. Saw nothing. Who could have gotten past the guards to even come onto the palace grounds?"

Cerise went to her. "What happened? Who do you mean?"

"You have not heard then. Oh, my poor girl, it is your cousin. Your cousin, the vicomte."

"Romain?" Cerise caught her breath. *No. Nothing could have happened to Romain.* All would be lost.

"It is true." Thérèse crossed herself. "Our Lord have mercy upon him."

Cerise sank down into the chair beside her, hands over her mouth. "He is dead?"

"Murdered," Thérèse breathed, crossing herself again. "Stabbed to death there in the stable yard and then thrown into the straw. They found him only this moment."

"No . . . no," Cerise said, half under her breath. "*No.*" She clung to Thérèse's hands, her breath coming with that same quick unevenness it had when she had spoken to Alexis mere moments ago. Had it been a premonition of death? "Who could have done it? Why?"

"Those murderous dogs, no doubt. Those rebels." Thérèse pulled Cerise protectively closer. "We are none of us safe!"

Cerise clung to her maid more tightly. No, it could not be. Alexis was one of them, but he said they wanted only justice and liberty. They would have no reason to kill Romain. He had harmed no one.

Take care. These are dangerous times, and one can never be certain who is to be trusted.

Oh, Alexis, how could you? What have you done?

"But why?" Cerise managed to ask at last. "Why should they kill him? What wrong had he done?"

Thérèse scowled. "The boy who found him, the gardener's boy, he said there was a paper stabbed through with the dagger that pierced his heart. He could not read it himself, of course, but he heard the guard speaking of it later. It was a notice to all aristocrats that the sins of the fathers shall be visited upon their children."

"But what does it mean? What had Romain's father done that Romain should be killed for it?"

"Oh, I do not know," Thérèse said. "I have never heard wrong about the vicomte's father, but perhaps it is an old grievance. Poor fellow, though. He was rather a coxcomb, but there was never any harm in him. And there was a priest murdered last night as well, not five miles from here. Truly, the world has gone mad."

Tears sprang to Cerise's eyes. "Oh, Thérèse, Thérèse, what am I to do now? I told Papa. I gave him my word! Now Sauveterre is gone to us."

"There now." Thérèse scooted her chair closer and pulled Cerise's head to her shoulder. "It cannot be helped now. And it may be all for the good. Not for poor Vicomte Lévesque, of course, but for you."

Cerise sniffed, trying to keep from crying. "What do you mean? Sauveterre is lost. I have nothing and no one. How can it be good?"

Thérèse clicked her tongue reprovingly. "You did not love Vicomte Lévesque. Be honest. You could never have loved him."

Cerise hid her face against Thérèse's neck. "It would have been a good match. I could have kept Sauveterre, and we would have gotten on well enough." She lifted her head. "At least he would have been kind to me. Now what am I to do? Go to the Comte de Therin-Toussant?" At that, her tears spilled over, and she clung to her maid, shaken with weeping.

"Shh, shh," Thérèse soothed. "There are other men in the world."

"None who will take me with no dowry."

"Nonsense, chérie. You are a lovely and good-hearted child. The man who loves you will ask no more than your sweet self. Anyone else is unworthy of you."

Cerise managed a watery laugh. "That is a very pretty thought, Thérèse. But it is not the way of the world. I could never live as the wife of a merchant or a banker."

Thérèse scoffed. "Truly, many of those are richer than our aristocrats. Where do you think all the money goes? To the wigmaker, the dressmaker, the shoemaker, and interest on money borrowed for wigs and clothes and shoes. Perhaps better a wealthy wine seller's wife than that of a poor duc, eh?"

Cerise sighed. Perhaps as a practical matter, Thérèse was right. Most of the nobles owed far more than could ever be repaid. The merchants and bankers grew wealthy on their extravagances. But that was not the point. Centuries of history were represented by those noble names. Centuries of noble blood flowed in those veins. Was it all to be forgotten? Her own father and mother came from such stock. Was she to betray them by mixing their proud blood with the blood of a common merchant? Perhaps a financier owned twice the wealth of a comte or duc, but his wealth could not ennoble his blood or the blood of his sons.

"Oh, Thérèse—"

There was a sharp knock at the door, and the maid went to answer it. Cerise could not hear her muted conversation. When Thérèse returned, she hurried Cerise to her dressing table.

"What is it, Thérèse?"

"You must go to the queen. She has sent one of her pages to fetch you at once."

"To the queen?" Cerise's brow furrowed. "Are you certain she has sent for me?"

"Do not be foolish. Of course I am."

"But why?"

Cerise shifted to look back at her maid, but Thérèse firmly turned Cerise's head forward again and piled her curls on top of her head.

"Do not ask me. I am the last one Her Majesty would explain herself to. And I was certainly not going to ask."

"But you know, don't you? Or *think* you know."

"I know I was told to see you were properly dressed for a private meeting with the queen on a matter of importance. It is not my place to know more."

Cerise watched her in the glass, wondering at the taut set of her mouth and the baleful look in her eyes as she straightened Cerise's black sleeve. For a long moment, the maid looked at her, searching for the tiniest flaw in her creation.

"Alas, chérie, you are perfection."

Cerise turned to her, taking her hands, eyes wide. "Thérèse, you're frightening me."

Thérèse pulled her hands free, her expression cold and stern. "Now is not the time to be afraid. Now is the time to consider what you truly wish to make of yourself. You might one day rise to be a great lady if you are willing to pay the price." Thérèse would say no more.

After a silent walk to the private salon, Cerise found herself in front of the queen. "You sent for me, Your Majesty?"

"Yes. Come in, child." The queen's face was worn with grief, though she held her head high. "Let me tell you some happy news."

Cerise smiled and curtsied. "Some happy news would be most welcome, my queen. There has been enough of the other kind."

"Yes, poor thing, we have had more than our share of sorrow, have we not? But you need not trouble yourself any longer. I know your father wished you to marry Romain so your son would one day inherit Sauveterre. But when Romain was killed, those lands passed to your cousin, Vicomte Leclerc."

Cerise looked at her, puzzled, trying to understand this new development. Could Sauveterre still be hers? "Yes, madame?"

"You need not worry about that any longer," the queen

said, smiling. "Your dear papa would have been most pleased."

"Oh, madame!" Cerise clasped her hands in front of her. "Is it possible that Sauveterre will still belong to my father's descendants?"

The queen managed a wan smile. "Oh, la, child, is it possible? Of course it is not possible. Your cousin has four grown sons, all of them married with sons of their own. It is they who shall inherit Sauveterre. But that is of no matter. I have found you a better match that will bring your father's descendants much more than his own title and holdings ever could have. Would he not prefer his eldest grandson be heir to the lands and title of a comte?"

"A comte, my queen? I do not—"

She broke off with a faint gasp. From behind the embroidered screen stepped the Comte de Therin-Toussant, his handsome lips curled into a self-satisfied smile.

"My very dear mademoiselle." The comte bowed and pressed a sensuous kiss to the back of her hand. "As I told Her Majesty, I have at last allowed my heart to overrule my head. I might have chosen from many ladies of great name and greater fortune, all of them a credit to my state. But, alas, how could I imagine any of them at my side when you might be there instead, outshining them all?"

She lowered her eyes as she knew any young lady ought when complimented, but it was not out of shyness or pleasure. She merely did not want him to see the panic that must have been plainly visible there.

"Monsieur," she said when she could trust her voice, "you do me great honor, but as you say, there are many ladies of higher station and more wealth who, I daresay, better deserve such attentions."

"But none I desire," he said, tilting her face up to him.

"You, ma belle, shall be mine as I always intended you would. Mine and no other's."

That burning intensity was again in his dark eyes, and she wished more than anything that she could snatch her hand away from him and run out of the room. But she could never do it. He was a comte and friend to the royal family. She would be ruined if she refused such a fine offer. Still, the match was a poor one for him. Surely the queen herself would wish to reward one of her political allies with such an honor.

Cerise managed a coy smile. "Monsieur trifles with me, I know. It cannot be that Her Majesty would approve of a marriage between someone so high and another so low. I am a worthy target of your sport, to be certain, monsieur, but not of such an honor."

"Your modesty becomes you, child," the queen said. "But you must not think less of yourself than is true. You are the daughter of a vicomte, are you not, and not a scullery maid. Besides, His Majesty and I wished to honor the comte for the great services he has done us these many months, but he would ask only one little thing. And how could I refuse him? There is so little joy in the world these days. How could I deny him something so simple?" Again she struggled to smile. "So, Gaspard, this pleases you at last?"

He made a deep, graceful bow. "It does, my dear queen. I have never minded overpaying for what I wish to have." He laughed lightly and helped himself generously from his snuffbox. "I have money enough, eh?"

Cerise looked at the box, her head whirling too much to really see it.

He laughed, mistaking her thoughts. "A rather pitiful thing compared to my usual box, is it not? Do not think this is an indication that my fortunes have fallen. The hinge on mine is broken, and I gave it to my fool of a valet to have it mended. I cannot say when I will have it again. This one will have to do for now."

Cerise barely took in the words.

The queen looked at her expectantly. "Have you nothing to say to the comte's gracious offer, child? Come, you will be the Comtesse de Therin-Toussant. Does that not please you? Of course it does. Well, you must let her alone for now, Gaspard. You have shocked the poor poppet." She waved one hand airily toward the door. "Take her back to her chamber and tell her maid to have her lie down with the room unlit and a perfumed cloth on her forehead."

"Gladly, dear queen," he said, returning the snuffbox to his waistcoat pocket. "But I will have an answer first."

"Do not be absurd, Gaspard," the queen said. "Of course she will be delighted to accept, will you not, child?"

Cerise clasped her hands together to keep them from trembling. That she despised the comte was no matter. That he looked at her as if she were a tender morsel to be devoured mattered even less. She was alone in the world. Her father's land and title had passed to another distant cousin. She lived here at court in luxury and plenty due to the queen's favor. If she refused the comte now, would not Her Majesty be offended and withdraw that favor? Then what was Cerise to do? She had never known anything but privilege. How could she survive alone and with nothing? Unless she were to sink to the lowest of trades, she would have to have a husband, and better one of wealth and position than any other.

Unbidden, she thought of Alexis, of the softness in his eyes and the gentle touch of his hands. Perhaps, as Thérèse had said, happiness lies in being loved and wanted. Well, she was wanted. The comte wanted her, as a miser wanted gold or precious gems, as a possession, no more. But loved?

Perhaps Alexis did love her. Perhaps she even loved him, but what did that matter? He was a poor man, a servant. How could he keep a wife? He would likely marry a girl of his own class, pretty and pert, no doubt, one who was handy with a lady's clothing and hair, and the two of them would stay in service together. Perhaps even to the Comte de Therin-Toussant and his comtesse.

Glancing at the comte and then away again, Cerise turned a half-hysterical laugh into a sigh. Perhaps Alexis was a murderer as well. She remembered the unsettled look on his face there in the roses and the hardness in his eyes when he spoke of an angel delivering her from marriage to Romain. Surely he would not go so far as murder. Oh, she didn't truly know. She didn't want to know. It didn't matter. Saint or devil, he was not for her. She had to have a husband who could provide for her in the midst of the madness that seemed to be everywhere. Why did it have to be so miserable a world?

She closed her eyes for a moment, gathering her courage. Then she lifted her head.

"Your Majesty is most gracious to consider one so unworthy. As is monsieur." She made a deep curtsy before the queen. "What can I do but accept with humble thanks?"

That fire burning bright in his eyes, the comte seized both of her hands and pressed them to his lips.

17

Palace of Versailles, France
June 1789

The next day, the comte again had business in Paris. Meanwhile, Cerise sat with the ladies of court, being told how fortunate she was to have been honored by the Comte de Therin-Toussant.

Thérèse looked grave and said very little. "The bed is made, chérie, and you, sadly, must now lie in it."

"Not until Noel," Cerise told her, but as Alexis had said, Noel would come.

She told herself she would not think of that. The agreement was made, and it was the will of the queen herself. It would be as it must. Still, Cerise found herself unable to sit quietly and work on the queen's embroidered bodice, the silver silk with tiny fleurs-de-lis worked in gold. Once again, she walked in the solitary parts of the garden accompanied by Thérèse, who kindly lagged behind or forged ahead to give Cerise her space. How often she had walked here with Alexis, but she never saw him now except for the briefest glance across a room or when he was hurrying after his master, seeing to his duties. And always, even when his face was set in the calm lines of an ideal servant, she could see that look in his eyes, the look of guilt, of regret, of horror. *Oh Alexis, what have you done?*

"Mademoiselle?"

She stopped walking, for the briefest instant thinking he

might be there behind her, but she knew she was wrong. That was not a man's voice but a boy's.

"Mademoiselle, if you please."

She turned to see the gardener's boy there, half-hidden by some bushes, looking terrified.

She smiled at him. "What is it, Michel? Come, you needn't fear. After what you did for me in the stables, I know I can count you as a friend. I am your friend as well. You knew I was there, did you not?"

He nodded. "I knew you did not wish to be seen, mademoiselle. I was glad to let them think it was me. But please, mademoiselle, I am afraid I will be hanged."

She nearly laughed, but there was genuine terror in the boy's eyes. "What is it, Michel? What have you done?"

"I swear it upon all the holy saints, mademoiselle, I did not steal it. I found it. I was going to keep it. To sell. Then I thought I would be found out. But I do not know how to return it without being thought a thief."

"What is it?" she asked. "What did you find?"

The boy pulled a ragged kerchief from his pocket and unwrapped an ornate snuffbox. It was the comte's.

"Where was this?"

The boy ducked his head. "In the stables, mademoiselle. Near . . ." He glanced up at her and then fixed his eyes on the ground once more. "Near where the gentleman was killed."

I gave it to my fool of a valet to have it mended. The comte had given the box to Alexis. No, it could not be, and yet now she was sure it was. *Alexis. Alexis, you fool!*

"I thought perhaps it belonged to the dead monsieur," the boy said. "I know it was wicked to take it, but he would not need it any longer. I made confession to our priest, and he said I must return it. Please, mademoiselle, can you not help?"

She took the box and stuffed it into her skirt pocket. "You have done right, Michel. Now you must go and tell no one of this." She glanced back at Thérèse, who was coming toward them, no doubt to make sure the boy was not making mischief. "Quickly now, you must go back to your work. Take this, petite, as thanks."

She slipped the gold ring off her little finger. It was a rather plain one, not expensive, but she had no money with her. She knew even so commonplace a piece of jewelry would be a great windfall for this poor boy.

"Oh, mademoiselle!"

"Go now. Hurry," she urged. "And tell no one."

He was gone before Thérèse reached them.

"Ma chéri!"

"Let me alone, Thérèse," she snapped. "I must think. Oh, I must think!"

It was proof that Alexis was guilty, was it not? Alexis hadn't wanted her to marry Romain. He had wanted to rescue her from "the popinjay." But this . . . this was murder. She had to report it. To the guard. To the king.

"Oh, Thérèse, what shall I do?"

The tale spilled out of her as she huddled there in her maid's arms.

"Speak to the comte about it," Thérèse advised. "If you are determined he is to be your husband, you must tell him everything. He will see to the matter for you."

Of course, that was the best way. When he returned from Paris, the next time they had a moment alone, Cerise would speak to him. God forgive her, she would.

It was later that same afternoon when the comte returned and sent a page with his invitation for Cerise to go driving with him. It would be the perfect opportunity for her to return the snuffbox and tell him what she knew about his valet. She would not bring up what Alexis had told her, his professed love and fidelity. It would be as well that the comte thought it was only the radical ideas Alexis had espoused that had driven him to murder an accursed aristocrat.

As they drove, Cerise found little opportunity to bring up so difficult a subject. The comte seemed quite content to carry most of the conversation, more charming and diverting than he had ever been before, and the time quickly passed. It seemed a very short while before they reached the bend in the road where they usually turned back toward the palace, but the carriage did not stop. It did not slow.

Cerise glanced at Thérèse and then at the comte. "Where are we going?"

He smiled at her, that smug little smile that clearly said he felt sure of himself. "I thought it best not to make things more complicated than they need be."

She looked out the window, feeling the carriage pick up speed. They were headed out of Versailles.

"Monsieur, where are we going?"

"As you know, ma belle, it is the wish of our beloved king and queen that we be married. It seems rather ungracious to delay the fulfillment of that wish, does it not?"

"Are you saying we are to be married at once?"

"It would save a good deal of trouble, ma belle, and your reputation."

Again Cerise glanced at Thérèse who sat beside her, lips pursed. "My reputation, monsieur? I do not know what you mean."

"Traveling with a man not your husband, chérie? La, the scandal."

Cerise felt a blush creep into her cheeks. "But the queen said—"

"The queen knows only that we have gone for our usual drive. It would not do to upset Her fair Majesty, would it?"

"But my things. The necessary papers. How can we—"

"That is all arranged, I assure you. I have permission from the king himself to travel from Versailles to London. He has so many things to deal with these days, I did not trouble him with the details, but his secretary was kind enough to include my betrothed and her maid in the documents. We will have no trouble leaving Calais."

"Calais?" Cerise gasped, and Thérèse took her hand.

"Monsieur le Comte," the maid scolded, "my lady cannot be stolen from the palace and from France as if she were so many francs or monsieur's lace handkerchief."

The comte looked down his nose at her. "You would do well, Madame Gossip, to remember your place and be thankful these papers say 'Mademoiselle Cerise Bélanger *and maid*.'"

Thérèse's eyes flashed, but she said nothing more.

"We are leaving *France*?" Cerise asked, trying not to sound as frightened as she felt. "Why?"

"Do not be a little goose, chérie. There is an ugly time coming. The people are angry, and they do not care now who knows it. The king himself has been urged to take his family and find refuge in another country, but the coward has delayed their flight again and again. Now even he is beginning to realize there will be bloodshed, peasant and noble. And not a mere drop here and there, but enough to fill the Seine."

Her heart pounded as she remembered Romain's murder and that of the priest and others whispered about in the palace, horrible and brutal and all in the name of justice. And she remembered the eyes of the peasants as the carriage rolled past them. "Dogs," the comte always called them. And too many of them, half-mad and ready to bite, looked it.

"Surely they would not—"

"I daresay there is no avoiding it now, but I do not intend to be here to witness it. I have sold everything but my land and estate and turned it all to gold. Before long, these so-called revolutionaries will be put back into their place, whether it is in the fields or in the grave, and then I will return for what is mine. Until then, we will take refuge in England, Comte and Comtesse de Therin-Toussant." He took her hand and pressed it to his lips, all the while looking into her eyes, smug and smiling. "Do not trouble yourself, ma belle. I know how to keep safe what is mine."

They drove fast, stopping at intervals to change horses but do little else. Cerise lost track of the hours. The heat was without pity, and the journey was almost dreamlike. No, it was more like a nightmare where the same thing happens again and again, tinged with foreboding, as if something terrible was to come.

As often as she pushed them aside, images of Alexis came back to her. How could she have thought she loved him? She still felt sickened when she realized what he and those revolutionaries had done. There was nothing noble about violence. Nothing idealistic about murder. For all his pretty words and pretty ways, he was very like the rabble that burned and looted and killed, he and his companions with their red, white, and blue cockades. *Beasts, all of them.*

She did not love the comte—she was well aware of that—but he would take care of her. He would see she was safe and comfortable even through these uncertain times. Alexis . . . well, obviously she was not as good a judge of men as she had thought. She shook her head, trying to rid her mind of the image of him speaking of liberty and equality, eager truth shining from his eyes. *Murderer,* she reminded herself. She had been foolish enough to toy with the idea that she might actually be in love with Alexis, and that merely proved the comte knew better than she had thought. Even if he were not a murderer and a rebel against the crown, Alexis was a valet, a peasant. There could never be a future for them together. Not in this world.

The comte rarely spoke except to tell the driver to hurry on, and at last they were in Calais, at an inn very near the docks.

"It is not so fine a place," he said as he handed her down from the carriage, "but after we have taken our dinner, I mean to sell the carriage and the horses. Come, everything should be prepared for us."

The innkeeper hurried out to meet them, smiling and red-faced. "Welcome, Monsieur le Comte! And mademoiselle, welcome! Come in! Come in! As your man requested, we have reserved our best parlor for your use until your ship sails."

He chattered on after that, leading them through a dingy front room to a slightly less dingy one in the back, but Cerise didn't hear him. *As your man requested*, he had said. *Your man.* Someone was bending over the table, setting the plates just so. She knew at once it was Alexis. *Must he be here?*

She slipped her hand next to the snuffbox in her skirt pocket as his eyes met hers.

He made a deep bow. "Mademoiselle. Monsieur le Comte. It is all prepared."

The comte sank into the chair Alexis was holding out for him, waving one hand to indicate Cerise should sit wherever she pleased. Alexis seated her across from his master and then served the thick stew and coarse bread. Cerise had no appetite for such plain fare, but the comte began to eat at once.

"Speak to the innkeeper," he told Alexis between bites. "Tell him I wish to sell the carriage and horses at once. I will give him a quarter of whatever price he gets for it if he can do it before we sail. And see the baggage is taken to the ship."

"Yes, monsieur." Alexis brushed Cerise's hand as he poured

her wine. Once again their eyes met. She read love in their velvet depths, love and pleading and urgency. *You need not marry him.*

She quickly looked away. *Idiot*, she scolded herself. *Will you be brought to ruin for a pair of dark eyes? a murderer's eyes? Oh, how could he do such things and seem so gentle?*

"Be quick, man," the comte scolded.

Alexis bowed. "At once, monsieur." He gave Thérèse a questioning look as he passed by her on his way to the door.

She merely pursed her lips and looked away.

Cerise was glad when he was finally gone. How she was going to bear seeing him still in his master's service after she and the comte were married, she did not know. No, once they were safely away, she would report what she knew to the comte. Then she need not worry any longer.

"Do you"—she took a sip of wine to wash the dryness from her throat—"do you mean for him to accompany us to England?"

The comte laughed. "To be sure, chérie. If one must go into exile, one ought to at least do so in style. He is a rascal, I have no doubt, but he looks well and knows not to speak out of turn, and there's no one to equal him for choosing my clothes. No, no, no. I cannot be without him and still hold my head up in society. We shall be a pretty little bit of domesticity, shall we not, with my valet and your crone there to look after us?" He laughed.

Thérèse stood at the door, hands folded, the picture of attentive service despite the flash of fire in her eyes. Clearly, she did not want the valet to go with them. Clearly, she wanted Cerise to tell the comte what she knew about Alexis and his confederates. Otherwise, might he not murder his master as well?

No, not in England, surely. In England he would be merely a valet. There was no rebellion there. There was no revolution. Besides, Alexis had in his way done the comte a service in removing Romain. The comte was as likely to reward him as report him.

Cerise glanced at Thérèse and almost imperceptibly shook her head. Better the comte not know. They were all leaving France and the past behind. The future was what mattered, and hers depended on the man sitting across the table from her.

You need not marry him. Even Thérèse had said so. *Happiness is not in wealth and privilege but in being loved and wanted.* Perhaps it was true. Cerise had herself seen much unhappiness between the married couples at court from infidelity, cruelty, and indifference. But was poverty and hardship something to be more desired?

Then she remembered a girl at the last place they had stopped, the innkeeper's daughter whose young husband was the hostler. She had a baby clinging to her skirts and another on the way, but she was as merry as spring. There was a special glow in her eyes whenever the hostler was in sight, a glow outshone only by the one in his eyes. If Cerise could be guaranteed that, perhaps the rest didn't matter. Ah, but there were no guarantees. Ask the king and the queen. Ask poor Romain.

She looked down at the simple food set before her and rubbed her throbbing temples. Thérèse had obviously changed her mind about Alexis and with good reason, but it didn't matter anymore. They would be in England in a few hours, and then Cerise would be married. She would forever belong to the Comte de Therin-Toussant. Whether it was hate or fear or love she felt, Alexis would never be anything but her husband's servant. To her, he would be nothing.

Nothing.

18

Cabot Falls, Vermont
Present Day

*S*ofia pressed her latest creation on the Pinot Painters, a tradition her two best friends seemed not to mind.

"Oh, how delicious," Marla said after one bite of delicate almond cookie. "What are these called?"

"Almond *tuiles*," Sofia told her, passing the plate to Julie. "What do you think?"

Julie sampled and rolled her eyes. "Divine. Though I'm surprised you have any extras with all your company. Actually, I'm surprised we had a chance to have our regular meeting."

Sofia helped herself to a cookie. "Jim, being the great husband he is, took everybody out to look at Christmas lights so we could paint."

"Are you going to serve these at the party you're catering?" Julie nudged Marla. "She's *catering* now, you know."

Sofia beamed. "Yes, I am. And yes, I am." She turned back to her painting, still smiling. "Oh, and I didn't tell you, but I talked to my Aunt Rachel and Aunt Louisa. They remembered the name of the French countess Nonna used to talk about. It was Cerise Valérian."

"Valérian?" Marla asked. "As in Gaspard Valérian, Comte Therin-Toussant?"

Sofia nodded. "The same. It would be too much of a coincidence if it wasn't."

Julie leaned back, shoulders drooping. "Drat. She married the comte? But she loved Alexis, didn't she?"

"She did," Sofia said, taking another cookie. "I'm sure she did."

"I guess she couldn't resist the comte's money and title." Marla helped herself to another one too. "And then she ended up with nothing anyway."

Julie sighed. "Maybe she couldn't imagine herself married to someone who wasn't nobility. She was used to being an aristocrat, after all."

Sofia considered for a moment. "Maybe we're looking at this the wrong way around. Maybe she *did* love him. Maybe she even wanted to marry him. But he was involved with those revolutionaries, remember? Maybe he was mixed up in something that eventually got him killed. Those were pretty risky times. He could have been put in prison or even executed by the government. Or even his friends could have turned on him. From what I've read, it happened a lot back then."

"Speaking of risky times," Marla said, "how are things going with the play?"

Sofia exhaled heavily. "We have rehearsal tomorrow, dress rehearsal the next night, and the play the night after, if the sets and costumes are still intact by then. After that, I'm taking a break from anything to do with the theater. For the next fifty years."

Marla laughed. "Have another cookie."

Apart from Connor and Jason whispering and Davy frequently excusing himself to go to the boys' room, rehearsal the next afternoon went smoothly. In spite of that, Naomi was more on edge than ever, snapping at every fault in the production, real or imagined.

Kenny seemed nervous too. More so than usual. And the harder he tried to be perfect, the worse he failed. Sofia, watching from the front for once, cringed when he stumbled over yet another line.

"No, Kenny," his mother said, her voice strident and overly patient. "It's 'second star to the right and *straight* on till morning.'"

He seemed relieved when he and the other children could finally leave the stage while Megan sang Wendy's new song. But after the first verse, Naomi stood up.

"Wait! Wait!" She shielded her eyes with one hand as she looked up at the stage lights. "Heather, what happened to the spotlight? It's supposed to be on Wendy while she's doing her song. Heather?"

There was some rattling around from up above. Then Heather's mop of red curls popped into view. "I'm sorry, Mrs. Moore, it went dead on me. I was trying to find the problem, but everything looks fine up here as far as I can tell. It should work, but it doesn't."

Jim popped his head out from behind the backdrop. "Want me to have a look?"

Naomi pursed her lips. "If you think you can get it working again, yes. As quickly as you can too, if you would, please. We're running out of time." She glanced at her watch. "Parents will be here in about thirty minutes."

"Right."

Jim disappeared. A minute later, he was up on the scaffold next to Heather. With the rest of the cast and crew, Sofia watched him tinker with the switch on the spotlight and then disappear again.

"Well, that'll do it." Jim reappeared from behind the backdrop holding a long loop of black electrical cord, the plug neatly severed. "Anyone know anything about this?"

Before anyone could do more than look baffled, there was a loud bang backstage and a yelp of pain.

"Kenny!" Her clipboard tossed aside for once, Naomi ran toward the noise. Sofia looked up at Jim and hurried after her, everyone else crowding behind them.

Kenny was sitting on the floor, his face contorted with pain as he tried to pull his left foot out from under Jim's toolbox. Jim immediately lifted the heavy box and set it down near the scaffolding.

"Are you all right?" Naomi dropped to her knees beside her son. "What happened?"

He squeezed his eyes shut, gritting his teeth. "My foot. I . . . I don't know how, but the box fell. From up there."

They all looked up at the scaffolding where Jim had been working. Sofia shot Jim a questioning glance, but he only looked puzzled and didn't say anything.

Kenny groaned and leaned against his mother when she put her arms around him, obviously not wanting anyone to see the tears standing in his eyes. "Mom, it really hurts."

"Okay, buddy," Jim said, kneeling at the boy's feet. "Can you wiggle your toes?"

Kenny tried and then grimaced. "No."

"All right." Jim tugged at the lace of his running shoe. "Let's have a quick look."

"Don't." Naomi glared at him. "This is your fault, Jim Parker. Don't think you can make it better by fussing over him now."

"What?" Sofia gasped. "How is this even remotely Jim's fault?"

Jim stood up, his expression grave but tightly controlled. "We'll discuss it later, Sofia. Right now, we need to get Kenny to the hospital."

"I can see to my own son," Naomi said. "Come on, Kenny. Put your arm around my waist."

Staring daggers into anyone who dared try to help, she managed to get the boy to his feet and guided him toward the back doors.

"And we certainly will discuss it later," she added as she opened the door, eyes flashing. "I will at least be discussing it with my attorney."

Kenny looked pleadingly toward Jim, more miserable than he was already. "Come on, Mom, it wasn't his fault. I'm sure the box just fell."

"Shh, come on now."

"Mom, Mr. Parker didn't—"

The doors swung shut behind them. The kids stood there in a little semicircle, not sure what to do. For a moment, no one said anything.

Mr. Trumbull appeared at the side of the stage, leaning on his push broom. "I guess that means you're done for the night, eh? Can't do much without your director and your star, I don't guess."

Sofia sighed. "Okay, everybody, let's get everything tidied up and put away. Your parents will be here pretty soon."

"Does this mean we don't have to do the play now?" Connor asked with a smirk.

She tried not to look too annoyed with him. "It means we're going to quit for tonight and figure out what to do once we know how Kenny is. Everybody on board with that?"

The kids murmured their assent and started clearing up, more than a few of them talking in whispers, no doubt about the latest incident. Sofia was putting away her supplies when she felt a tug at her sleeve.

"Mrs. Parker?"

Davy Reid looked a little uncertain, but there was also a touch of eagerness in his eyes. "Yes, Davy?"

"I was wondering, um, if you thought I should work on my lines tonight. I mean, in case."

She glanced at Jim, who was repacking his toolbox and listening in.

"Well, that is an understudy's job, isn't it?" she said a touch more brightly than she meant to. "We won't know for a while how Kenny is, or if he'll be able to be in the play. We'll have to see what happens." She looked at him for a moment, watching his eyes. "Did you see what happened to Kenny? I didn't see you out front with the other boys. I thought maybe you might have seen something."

Davy shook his head, his face reddening. "I, uh, had to go. You know?"

Sofia nodded. "I understand. Are you feeling all right?"

He gave her a sheepish grin. "I think I drank too much soda all at once."

"That'll do it. Well, you'd better get your things. Your mom will be here in a minute."

"Okay." He walked away and then turned back. "Sorry about Kenny. Do you think he'll be all right?"

"I think so," she told him.

Davy shook his head and then sprinted away.

"Are you sure you couldn't have left the toolbox too close to the edge?" she asked Jim when they were alone.

He shook his head. "I'd finished tightening all the screws that hold the block and tackle. I had the toolbox right in the middle of the scaffolding, as far away from the edge as it could be."

Sofia pressed her lips together. "Then it couldn't have fallen accidentally."

"And there's this." He pulled the tape measure out of his pocket. "It was over there, under that bench. I almost didn't see it."

She took it from him, wishing it could tell her what had happened to Kenny. "It couldn't have fallen out when the box hit the stage?"

"The box was still closed after it hit. Those latches are hard to open and shut. There's no way."

She frowned, considering. "Are you sure it was in the box in the first place?"

"Absolutely. I used it to measure one of the supports, and then I clipped it back in the holder." He opened the toolbox and showed her the empty space among all the gadgets stored in the lid. "Like I said, I was done for the night. I had everything put away and closed up tight. Someone took it out. Had to have." He glanced up at the scaffolding. "And someone moved the toolbox."

She didn't like what she was thinking. "I suppose someone could have wanted to use the tape measure and moved the toolbox when he borrowed it and didn't realize he'd left it so close to the edge up there." She winced a little, knowing how lame that explanation sounded. "And forgot to put the tape measure back."

"Come on, Sofia. With everything that's been happening around here, do you really think this was an accident? Somebody wanted to put our star out of commission. I'm glad it landed on his foot and not his head."

"Me too." She looked at the tape measure still in his hand. "Too bad we didn't get it dusted for fingerprints or something."

He grinned a little. "There would have been plenty of fingerprints. Mostly mine. Then Naomi would really have had a fit."

"It would have been great evidence for her lawsuit anyway." Sofia shook her head. "She can't really mean to sue us, can she? Over this? It was an accident. Well, not an accident, but still not your fault."

"You might have trouble convincing the police of that. Yeah, somebody has obviously been causing trouble around here, but we don't have any proof of who it could be. As much as we suspect this is part of it all, we don't have any proof of that either."

"If this wasn't an accident," Sofia said, "what did the tape measure have to do with it? Why would our little mischief-maker have taken it out and left it behind?"

"Yeah." He nodded toward the bench. "Especially over there." He put his arm around her. "Come on, honey. We've had enough drama for one night. Whoever's doing all this has to give himself away before long. Just wish we knew why."

She leaned into Jim, returning the hug. "Poor Kenny. None of this has turned out very well for him, has it?"

"Well, I'm fairly sure his foot is broken, maybe in more than one place. But it looked like a clean break. There probably won't be any complications. At least I hope there won't be."

"Me too. Maybe if it's not too bad, Naomi will calm down and forget about this whole lawsuit idea."

Jim snorted. "I guess we can hope."

Sofia sighed. "Well, it is the season of miracles."

19

*C*erise stood at the dock, looking up at the ship that would carry them across the channel to England. She was holding the comte's arm but barely listening as he spoke to the innkeeper.

"That is all. I beg your pardon, monsieur," the man said. "He will pay not a sou more."

"It is worth ten times that!" the comte raged.

"But he says there is no market for such things these days. He doubts he can ever sell it again."

"The beasts alone are worth more." The comte swore and then motioned to Alexis, who was coming down the gangplank. "Attend to mademoiselle while I see to this imbecile who wishes to steal my carriage and horses."

Alexis quickened his step and then bowed before him. "Yes, monsieur. And the luggage is all settled. We need only go aboard."

"Very good. Now, innkeeper, take me to this dog who would rob me before my face." The comte stalked off with the innkeeper scurrying after him, struggling to match his long strides.

Alexis came to Cerise's side. For a long time they both stood watching the tossing sea and saying nothing. She hardly dared speak for the tumult inside herself and for the fear it would sound in her voice. And then she thought perhaps she should show him she did not care. Whatever he had said or thought, whatever he had done, he was merely a servant. She would soon be a comtesse.

"Where is Thérèse?" she asked, her voice cool and impersonal.

He smiled slightly, as if he knew what she was trying to do. "Forgive me, mademoiselle, but she would not allow me to take your things aboard. She insisted on seeing to them herself."

She nodded, still looking out to sea and listening to the rush of the tide, the squawking birds, and the sounds of the sailors preparing to cast off.

"You need not go with him," Alexis murmured when she said nothing more.

She ignored the stifling tightness in her throat and made her expression coldly serene. "Of course I must go with him. We are to be married. It is the queen's desire."

"The queen has more to worry her than you," he said, and there was an odd touch of pity in his eyes. "Perhaps, and sooner than we might think, France shall have no queen."

"Hush," she hissed. "I will not hear treason spoken."

"Not treason. Merely grim reality."

"Because of men like your friends? Bloodthirsty beasts, and you no better than they, for all your fine words."

He winced. "Do you think so of me? Truly? Even now?"

"Should I not?" she cried, and then she glanced behind herself, making sure the comte had not yet returned. "Should I not?" she asked again, lowering her voice. "You and those animals murdered Romain."

His eyes widened. "What?"

She seized the ornate snuffbox from her skirt pocket and thrust it into his hands. "This was there, beside his body. And I know the comte had given it to you to have it mended."

"No," he breathed, shaking his head. "That is not so. I never had it."

"Do not trifle with me. I saw your face the next day and all the days afterward. You dared not even look at me for shame."

"I . . ." That look came once more into his eyes, the look of guilt and shame that had been there the night Romain was murdered. "No, mademoiselle, it was not I, nor was it any of my confederates. They were pleased to take the credit for it, I do not doubt, to add to the terror of their reputation. But we were not there when the vicomte was killed."

She narrowed her eyes. "No? Then where were you? What did you mean when you said you feared the innocent would suffer in what was to come?"

He looked away from her now, not allowing her to see his face at all. "I was with them that night," he said, his voice soft. "I do not deny it. They told me they were only going to speak to him, to convince him to take our part, to speak on behalf of the people."

"Romain? He would never have—"

"No. Not him. The priest, Frère Baudouin." Tears sprang into his eyes and warped his voice. "In God's name he begged them to stop, to consider what they were doing, to speak for peace and justice, not violence. And Dupont"—he took a half-choked breath—"Dupont came up behind him and cut his throat, before his altar with his rosary in his hand. 'There is your peace, priest,' he said, and then—"

"Oh, Alexis!" She clasped both of his hands in hers, and he clung to them.

"I do not remember what then, except I came back to the palace and did not return to them again. I can never go back. They soil the very name of liberty with innocent blood."

"Then you did not kill Romain?"

"No." He shook his head and gave the snuffbox back to her. "No. Whoever it was, it was not I or anyone I know of."

"They will kill you if they think you have betrayed them," she breathed, concealing the box in her pocket once more, too relieved to know he was innocent to be concerned about anything else. "Is that not so?"

"It is. So you see, I, too, must become an émigré. That is one of the reasons I came with Monsieur le Comte now." He managed hint of a smile. "But only one."

He looked around and then hurried her into the narrow alleyway between two buildings, squeezing the hand he still held.

She felt her heart break. "Alexis, no. No, no, no." She forced a smile. "We have had a very pretty little flirtation, but you know it can never be more. It is no use torturing ourselves with sentiment when that is the truth."

"It is only the truth if you allow it to be."

She looked into his eager eyes, hardly knowing what to think. "I . . . I would not know what to do. I would not know how to live! Alexis—"

"The world is changing, ma belle. Even my master knows this, else why would he be leaving all he has?"

"But he will come back for it. The people will calm themselves, and order will be restored. Then we will live as we were meant to live."

"You cannot know that. You have seen what it is like in Paris. It is so in all of France. Things will never truly be as they once were. The comte may escape with what he has with him, but no more than that. Would you face life with a man you do not love—no, a man you *despise*—who cannot even provide for you?" He caught an unsteady breath. "Cerise, ma belle, would you not rather face this new world with someone who loves you more than his own life? Someone, I dare wager, you also love?"

He pressed her hand to his warm lips, his eyes pleading now. Her own spilled over tears. *Oh, bon Dieu, how do I know what to do? what to choose?* There could never be a future for them together. Not in this world.

She tightened her hold on his hand. Not in *this* world, but if this world was vanishing . . .

"Alexis—"

"*Cochon!*" The comte struck Alexis across the shoulders with his walking stick. "Filthy swine! Dare you lay hands on my lady!"

With a little cry, Cerise shrank back against the rough brick of the alleyway wall. Alexis staggered at the blow. As the comte raised the stick again, Alexis seized it and wrenched it away from him.

"I'll have you whipped, cur!" the comte snarled, but he took a step back.

Alexis held the stick in both hands, grasping it as if he had to force himself not to use it on its owner. "No, Monsieur le Comte, I pray you pardon me. I think it wise for me to leave your service and try my fortune elsewhere."

The two men stood there, wary and out of breath.

Then the comte laughed. "Go then. To the devil if you like. I haven't time to deal with you as you deserve. Come, Cerise."

Cerise froze where she was. *Bon Dieu, what should I do?*

"Now, mademoiselle. The tide will not wait for us." The comte took a step toward her.

Alexis stepped between them, the walking stick still in his hands. "No, monsieur, the lady will not go with you except by her own choice." He looked at her, still a gentle entreaty in his eyes.

The comte sneered at him. "You've let this talk of equality go to your head. Do you think this lady, any lady, would stoop to anything more than flirtation with a baseborn dog such as you? A valet? When she has, by the queen's grace, been betrothed to one so far above her?" He held out his hand. "Cerise, come with me *now*."

For a moment, no one moved.

Then Alexis stepped back and offered his own hand. "It is for you to choose, mademoiselle."

The comte snorted. "As if the minx had sense enough to make such a choice. Did not Her Majesty choose for you, girl? Would not the queen of all France be wiser than a little coquette whose head is as empty as her purse? Your father is dead. His lands and titles have gone to another. You have nothing without me, girl. You *are* nothing without me. Now come. Before I decide I have given you my favor unwisely."

She felt the blood flame into her cheeks. Eyes stinging, she glanced at Alexis. He was white with fury.

"Monsieur does himself no credit, speaking so of a lady."

The comte looked him over coldly. "And you are a fool if you think your opinion is of the least interest to me. If you wish to go, go. But you will not be taking with you what is mine."

He took hold of Cerise's arm, pulling her toward the dock, but Alexis stood in his way.

"Only if it is *her* choice, monsieur."

"Out of my way," the comte ordered, trying to shoulder past him.

Alexis pushed him back. "No, monsieur."

The comte laughed, startled, incredulous. "Dare you lay hands on *me*?" He struck Alexis across the face, bloodying his cheek with the ringing blow.

"No!" Cerise pulled free of the comte and ran to Alexis, pressing her handkerchief to his face as she grasped the lapel of his coat. "Take me with you. I do not care where we go, but I cannot go with him."

"You choose him? A valet? A peasant?" The comte swore. "I see this is no recent passion. You've been dallying with him all along." He barked a harsh laugh. "And to think I sent him to find out who at court had caught your attention. But it is of no matter. You are mine."

"No. I cannot, I *will not* marry you." Her heart pounded inside her, but she lifted her chin and looked directly into his eyes. "I love Monsieur Dieudonné."

She clung to Alexis's arm, waiting for the comte's reaction.

He merely shrugged. "That, mademoiselle, is of no interest to me. You are mine. I killed a nobleman in order to make it so. Do you think I will allow this impertinent dog of a valet to stand in my way now?"

She caught a quick breath. "*You* murdered Romain?"

The comte gestured toward Alexis. "He and his rebel friends will not mind that I assisted them in ridding France of another useless aristocrat, eh?"

"You killed him." She took the snuffbox from her pocket and held it out to him with trembling hands. "It was you who murdered him in cold blood."

He lifted one eyebrow and then, smiling, took the box from her. "Ah, there it is. I suppose I dropped it in the stable. Would you like to hear the use I made of it, girl? Shall I tell you how your fair cousin came riding in, still reeking of the tavern he'd been in that night? The stableman had already told me the Vicomte Lévesque had gone out late, so I knew he would come back before true dawn. Before he could call the boy to take his horse, I stopped him. He was rather surprised to see me, but that did not keep him from making one of his little pleasantries and calling me Monsieur Dariole. We were both terribly amused by that."

Cerise glanced at Alexis standing stone-faced at her side.

"I complimented him on his wit," the comte continued, "and offered him some of my snuff. Smiling as was always his way, he took some. 'You know, Monsieur Dariole,' he said, 'you are a good fellow and not so overproud as I have thought. I shall not make such sport of you from this moment forward.' I smiled and watched him for a moment, steadying him when he suddenly stumbled. 'No, monsieur,' I said as I helped him into the stable, 'I am most certain you shall not.'"

"What did you do to him?" Cerise breathed.

The comte smiled coldly and put the snuffbox into his coat pocket. "The snuff was a particular blend I use on special occasions. It does not kill, only stupefies. It was nothing for me to lay the worthy vicomte in the straw and tell him all the wrongs he had done me before I drove my poniard into his heart. It was an amusement I had promised myself for some while now, and I found it extremely satisfying."

Cerise had to force herself not to tremble at his dispassionate description. "But what had he done? He meant no one any harm."

"He stood in my way. You were determined to have him, fool that he was, and that was not my desire. I had hoped that Mademoiselle Plamondon, whom the queen wanted for him, would put him out of play, but she was much more willful than I would have expected from the look of her. That left me to see to matters myself, and this . . ." he said, his eyes and teeth gleaming in the gathering shadows. "This brought me great pleasure."

"Murderer," she whispered, clinging more tightly to Alexis's arm. "God forgive you the wickedness you have done."

"These are desperate times, mademoiselle. God has his own business to see to. For myself, I haven't the leisure to play games with you and your bibelot there. The ship will be leaving any moment, and you will be with me on it."

He grabbed her arm and pulled her forward. She stumbled to her knees in the dirty, wet alley. Alexis was on him with a low growl, shoving him away from Cerise and striking him two hard blows to the midsection.

The comte spat out an oath, pulled a dagger from the sheath

hidden inside his coat, and slashed at Alexis. Alexis raised the walking stick, swinging it to ward off the blow. But the comte ducked, too quick for him, and it snapped in two on the iron lamppost. The comte sprang again, but Alexis threw down the remains of the walking stick and caught him by the wrist, both hands holding the weapon away from him. The older man threw all his weight behind the blade, adding his other hand to better his grip. They stood there locked in the struggle, too alike in size and build for either to have an advantage.

Cerise shrank against the alley wall, afraid to move, afraid to cry for help. Alexis would be arrested, and he would be hanged for daring to strike a nobleman, for daring to strike his master. She would still be taken on the ship, away from the man she loved, bound forever to one she hated. A murderer. And Alexis . . .

She threw herself at the comte, dragging his arm down, turning the dagger away from Alexis. Panting and sobbing, she clung to him as he threw Alexis aside and turned on her, white flecks on his lips and his face purple with rage.

"Have it as you will, strumpet," he rasped, raising the blade as she shrank from him, as she shielded herself with bare and useless hands.

20

Calais, France
June 1789

The comte hurtled toward Cerise as the knife slashed downward.

She squeezed her eyes shut, sobbing out a prayer. The impact of his body threw her against the wall, and she tumbled into a heap on the ground. He gave a gasping groan as his whole weight fell against her.

She froze, waiting for the final blow.

He did not move again.

When she looked up, she realized Alexis was leaning against his master's back, his arms wrapped around the comte's body, his hands covering the comte's hands over the hilt of the dagger—the dagger that was now buried in the comte's chest.

In another moment, Alexis shoved the body off of her and pulled her up into his arms. "Cerise, mon ange, are you hurt?"

He held her back from him, looking her up and down, then pulling her close again. She clung to him, shaking and sobbing.

"He was going to kill you. I could not let him." Her breath caught. She looked up at him, round-eyed. "Oh, Alexis."

He nodded and then dropped to one knee beside the body, bowing his head.

"Mon chér." She pulled him to his feet, shaking him by the shoulders. "You must go. Run. You cannot stay here."

"I have nowhere to go," he said. "I have killed the Comte de Therin-Toussant. There is no place in France safe for me now.

Cerise . . ." He wrapped his arms around her, held her tight, and kissed her, kissed her with all the passion that had before been only in his eyes. "Go now. Run for the watch. You must tell them I killed the comte. If you do not, they will think you were in it with me, and you, too, will hang. Hurry, before we are found."

"No." She clung to him.

"You must! Don't be a fool!"

"I won't." She realized she was still crying, but she didn't care. "I won't leave you. Not now. Let them find us. I don't care."

"Mon amour." He embraced her. "Don't be a fool," he repeated, this time soft and low. To her ears, it seemed the sweetest of endearments. "For my sake, I beg you, do as I say."

She looked at him, eyes brimming with tears. Then, unable to speak, she nestled against him once more.

"Cerise," he murmured, holding her close. "Don't make this harder than it already is. Please, go now. Call the watch. It is the only way."

"Cerise!"

They both gasped, turning to see Thérèse standing at the opening to the alley.

Thérèse hovered there, a coat over her arm and her mouth in a hard line as she looked at the body sprawled on the wet ground. "You must do as he says," she said. "Monsieur is right. You will be seen as his accomplice if you do not call the watch. Even in defense of his own life, even in defense of a lady, a valet can expect nothing but hanging if he kills his master."

Cerise did not loosen her hold on Alexis's coat. "Thérèse, no."

"But," the maid continued, "if a nobleman were to strike his servant, his insufferably insolent servant, I doubt there would be anyone to question it."

Alexis shook his head. "What are you saying, madame?"

"Quickly, monsieur. Put this on." She handed him the coat, a pale blue brocade. "It is one of the comte's. The innkeeper's boy brought it, and I was taking it to the ship. It was mistakenly left behind at the inn. Quickly now!"

Cerise laughed suddenly, feeling a trifle hysterical. "Oh, yes. Alexis, hurry!"

She removed the comte's wig, careful not to touch him, careful not to think too deeply about what they were doing, and put it on Alexis as he slipped into the coat. It took her but a moment to arrange it properly. Already he looked like an aristocrat.

Thérèse swiftly removed the comte's many rings and the diamond pin from his jabot. Just as swiftly, Alexis put them on. Then he turned out the comte's pockets and took his money and papers.

Thérèse looked him up and down. "The breeches will have to do." Then she curtsied. "Monsieur le Comte."

Alexis looked a trifle pale, but he knelt beside the body and wrestled off the bloodstained cherry-colored coat, replacing it with his own plain one. Then he looked up at Thérèse.

"What else?"

"Give me that." Thérèse found a short length of rusty chain in the alley and bundled it in the coat, tying the sleeves around it to keep it all in place. Then, with a quick look to make sure she was unobserved, she stepped out onto the dock and dropped the bundle into the water.

"The snuffbox," Cerise gasped, but her maid only pursed her lips.

"It's gone to the bottom with the rest. If it's ever seen again, it will be too late to matter. Now, drag him over near the ship. If he bleeds out in the alley, there will be questions."

Alexis did as she bade him, swift and silent.

Thérèse rubbed her hands together and then put them on Cerise's shoulders. "Now, chérie, what is it we tell the watch? Hurry now, before they come and find us."

Cerise glanced at the body of the Comte de Therin-Toussant sprawled there on the dock and licked her dry lips. "I must tell them that this man is Alexis Dieudonné, the valet of my betrothed."

"Yes, and?"

"And?" Cerise looked helplessly at her and then at Alexis.

He took her hand. "He insulted you with his attentions, yes? And then struck me." He touched his cheek and managed a faint, grim smile. "That much at least is true."

"Yes."

"And then what, chérie?" Thérèse prompted. "Quickly!"

"And then he attacked Monsieur le Comte, who was forced to kill him."

She said it quickly, trying her best to keep her voice from shaking. Alexis squeezed her hand.

"It will be all right, mon ange, so long as we do not lose our courage. In such a matter, they will expect you to be upset. Just hold to our story, no matter—"

"What is this, monsieur?"

Three men stood at the end of the dock, two of them with pikestaves, one with a stout club in his belt. Cerise looked helplessly at Alexis as they drew closer.

"The watch at last, and a fine time you've been about it!" Thérèse stormed up to them as she scolded. "My lady and her betrothed, the Comte de Therin-Toussant, as good as murdered, and you filling your bellies with wine, no doubt. Sacré bleu!"

The three men looked at one another. The one with the club nudged the body with the toe of his worn boot and then made a slight bow.

"Pardon, monsieur, we did not know. We were on the other side of the tavern and heard the sounds of a struggle. And now, well, pardon, but the man is dead. It is our duty to . . ."

The second man elbowed him when he faltered.

"Pardon," the first man began again, "but you are the Comte de Therin-Toussant?"

Alexis turned to him, his face suddenly cold and disdainful. "Surely you have heard of me."

"We have." The third man looked him up and down, not quite threatening with his pikestaff. "Your papers, Monsieur le Comte."

Muttering to himself, Alexis patted his coat and brought out the king's permit. "I suppose you read?"

The man snatched the papers from him, narrowing his eyes as he looked them over. Then he looked at Cerise. "Your name, mademoiselle?"

"Cerise Bélanger."

He squinted at the page again.

The first man snatched it from him. "I'll see to this. Cerise Bélanger," he repeated as he studied the paper, his lips slowly moving as he made out each word.

"There, man," Alexis said, pointing out the place where the names were listed. "There. Mademoiselle Cerise Bélanger."

The watchman scratched his unshaven chin and nodded at Thérèse. "And that one?"

"Her maid," Thérèse huffed, hands on hips. "Surely you would not expect a lady of quality to travel without one."

Again the man studied the paper. "Says maid *and* valet. This one here?"

"Yes." Alexis pulled the lace handkerchief from his coat pocket and fluttered it in the direction of the body. "That cur dared to insult my lady with his attentions. Then when I reprimanded him for it, he had the temerity to strike me. See here!" He turned his face to display the darkening bruise on his cheek, and then patted it with the handkerchief. "It is unpardonable."

"The Comte de Therin-Toussant, eh?" said the third man. "And his name?"

"Dieudonné. Alexis Dieudonné."

The men of the watch exchanged glances.

"Alexis Dieudonné," said the third man, his expression suddenly sly and almost gloating.

"He has been in my employ for many years now," Alexis said, sneering at the body. "And yet I see he is a rogue and a villain. No doubt in league with those who would have us ruled by idlers and peasants."

"Could be, I suppose." The man's laugh was nastier than his grin. "Well, I'd say we're well rid of those who cannot be trusted."

The first man frowned at him. "Not so quickly, Dupont. Forgive us, monsieur, but you must go to the magistrate. After all, the man *is* dead."

Alexis huffed. "Delays, delays, we cannot have them. The tide will not wait. This is quite a simple matter, no? The man attacked me. See there!" He pointed to the broken cane next to the body. "My own walking stick. The dog dared strike me over the shoulders. I merely defended myself."

"But the magistrate—"

"The magistrate has enough to trouble him as it is, does he not?"

With only a hint of a smile, Alexis produced three gold coins and slipped one into each man's hand. Seeing they did not protest, he shoved the body with one foot and let it roll into the water. There was a heavy splash and then nothing.

"Now, the magistrate has no trouble at all, yes?"

The first two men looked rather uncertain, but the third put his arms around their shoulders.

"Why worry the magistrate? This Dieudonné was a rogue, no doubt. He's been seen to as any peasant ought who dares strike his master, eh? And we, my pretty ones, we shall have our fill of wine, courtesy of the good comte. Who are we to complain?"

"Excellent." Alexis tossed the broken stick after its owner and dusted off his hands. "Now that we have come to so fair an agreement, I will wish you fine fellows a good evening. Mademoiselle?"

Cerise took his arm, holding tight to steady her trembling hands. Surely they could see. Surely they knew.

Alexis led her past them, down the dock and toward the ship, Thérèse hurrying behind them. Cerise felt the blood pounding in her head as they walked. Slowly, so slowly. Why did he have to walk so slowly?

"Courage," he murmured to her when they heard footsteps behind them.

"Monsieur le Comte. A moment." It was the man with the sly eyes.

Cerise tightened her hold. "Al—"

Alexis squeezed her hand to silence her. Then he turned, again with that icy disdain. "What is it, man? My ship will sail."

The watchman made a slight bow. "Mademoiselle's glove, if you please."

"Ah."

He handed the glove to Cerise. "There, ma belle, you must have dropped it."

Alexis gave the man another coin, and the villain touched his battered hat.

"Merci, monsieur. Among my fellows it is counted a favor to see a traitor meet a bad end. I have a cousin in Versailles who will enjoy the tale I will have for him when next we meet."

"Well then"—once more, Alexis gave him money—"tell your cousin to drink deep, courtesy of the Comte de Therin-Toussant. And tell him Alexis Dieudonné is no more."

"Monsieur," the man said with another grin and another bow, "he will be pleased at the news."

Cerise looked away, not wanting him to see the fear in her eyes as once more they strolled toward the ship.

"Alexis," she whispered, "he was wearing one of those red, white, and blue—"

"Shh. The ship will be leaving soon. Just go. Do not look back."

All around the ship there was activity, sailors preparing to set sail, passengers hurrying to board, friends and family bidding them farewell, knowing it might be some while before they met again.

Cerise stopped before she stepped on the gangway herself.

"Come, ma belle," Alexis urged. "He is still watching. No doubt he would like to slide a blade into the heart of Monsieur le Comte, the cursed aristo, but at least he will tell all those of his confederacy that there is no need to look for the traitor Alexis Dieudonné. Come, we mustn't stop."

"It is the last time," she said, feeling a piercing pain in her heart, "perhaps the very last time I will ever set foot in France."

He held more tightly to her hand.

She looked back toward Paris, toward Versailles. Then she wiped her eyes with her free hand. "Alexis—"

"Hurry now."

She glanced back once more, and Thérèse fixed her with a stern eye. It was enough to make Cerise turn around again, head held high, and on her face a look of cool indifference to match her escort's.

"I am the Comte de Therin-Toussant," Alexis said to the first mate. "My valet was to have made all the arrangements for me and my betrothed."

"Oh, certainly. We were informed of your coming." The mate bowed. "I will inform the captain of your arrival."

"I fear the France we know will soon be no more," Alexis murmured when he was gone. "I had hoped in some way I might help bring justice and freedom to our country for peasant and noble alike. But it seems that can never truly be so in this world. Yet one day, and I pray it will be soon, perhaps there will be peace."

They looked across the channel toward England and the future, and she tightened her hold on his hand.

"May le bon Dieu make it so."

21

Cabot Falls, Vermont
Present Day

$\mathcal{B}$efore she had a chance to talk herself out of it, Sofia jumped into the Suburban and drove to the address she had gotten online. Naomi lived only a few blocks from the school, and the drive was long enough to give Sofia a chance to rehearse what she wanted to say. There had to be a way to work things out without a lawsuit.

She parked in front of the Moore home, a small tract house in the middle of the block, neatly kept but unremarkable. A wobbly line of unlit Christmas lights framed the door and windows. There was a boy's bicycle lying on its side in the front yard and an overturned sled on the porch next to some potted roses. Sofia was glad to see a light on in the front room. It wasn't even eight o'clock yet, but she knew some people went to bed early. Even if it wasn't her habit, Naomi was probably worn out with everything that had happened. Sofia wouldn't have blamed her for crashing early.

Steeling herself, she tapped on the door, not too loudly in case someone was already in bed. When no one answered, she knocked again, this time a bit louder. Finally she heard footsteps and someone turning the deadbolt. Naomi stood in the doorway looking at her warily.

"Uh, hi, Naomi. I'm sorry to come over without telephoning. I really hate when people do that, but I was afraid you wouldn't talk to me if I called you on the phone."

Naomi raised one eyebrow.

Sofia suddenly felt foolish and nestled a little deeper into her coat. "I thought maybe we could discuss things for a minute. Uh, inside?"

For a moment, Naomi stood there, pursing her lips. Then she sighed and stood back from the doorway.

"Kenny's sleeping, just so you know."

Sofia nodded. "I'll be quiet, and I won't stay long. How is Kenny?"

"His foot is broken. Come sit down."

Sofia followed Naomi into the den and sat on the pristine cream-colored sofa. It was a pleasant enough room, a little out-of-date but meticulously decorated and very neat. More like a furniture store showroom than a home. There was no Christmas tree, nothing but a little string of pine garland over the fireplace and one stocking.

Naomi sat in a straight-backed chair next to the sofa. "I'm sure your husband didn't intentionally leave that toolbox where it was going to hurt someone, but it was negligent of him all the same."

Sofia exhaled heavily. "Naomi, Jim and I are very sorry about what happened. You don't know how much Jim's been beating himself up over the accident, about his toolbox hurting Kenny and wondering how it could possibly have fallen. We're very fond of Kenny, and we'd never want to see him hurt. But you can't really believe Jim's responsible. There have been some strange things going on in the auditorium. I'm not saying this is connected to that necessarily—"

Naomi's eyes flashed. "Are you saying it wasn't an accident?"

"I'm saying I don't know what happened. But I know Jim didn't do anything that could have been a hazard to those kids. Come on now. You don't really think this is worth a lawsuit, do you?"

"My attorney does."

Sofia blinked, stunned by her matter-of-fact tone. "You've already hired an attorney?"

"I wanted to know what my options were. He's very optimistic about our chances of prevailing in the suit."

"You mean he's very optimistic about charging you a lot of money to pursue a very iffy case."

"I suppose a judge will have to decide how strong the case is." Naomi smiled coolly. "I'll take my chances. I can guarantee you I'm not going to forget the matter."

"Naomi, we're neighbors. I thought we were friends. Can't we talk this out? Why does there have to be a lawsuit?"

Naomi snorted softly. "If there's one thing I've learned, it's if you don't stand up for yourself, the other guy will walk right over you."

"Nobody is trying to walk over you!" Sofia glanced toward the hallway and then lowered her voice. "Why do you always have to be so hard to talk to?"

"Me?" Naomi frowned. "That's not true. Anyone can talk to me about anything. I'm always willing to listen."

"You're willing to listen, but nobody is willing to tell you the truth."

Naomi's frown deepened. "What do you mean?"

"I mean they're all afraid to tell you how they really feel, but I know some of the kids are on the verge of quitting. They have been almost the whole time. I've been wondering if these incidents at the auditorium weren't a kind of protest, you know?"

Naomi's eyes flashed. "A protest? Against me?"

"I'm not saying that's necessarily the case," Sofia said. "But if you don't start treating them better, they'll eventually rebel against you, and then there won't be a play. Just look at Kenny."

"What about Kenny? Are you saying my own son is afraid of me? Don't be ridiculous."

Sofia steeled herself and then plunged ahead. "He doesn't want to be in the show. Everybody knows it but you."

"Nonsense. Of course he does. He loves it. You heard him say so yourself."

"You heard his words, Naomi, but you didn't hear what the rest of him was saying. You didn't see the unhappiness in his eyes or the defeat in every line of his body. He's a good little actor, he really is, but even he couldn't conceal that. Not from anyone who was paying attention."

"What are you saying? That he was lying to me?"

Sofia shrugged a little, hating that she had to say any of this. "Not lying, not really, but telling you what he thought you wanted to hear. I know he loves you. Obviously he wants to please you, but he doesn't want to be in the show. He'd rather help Jim with the sets. I'm sure it's been hard for him since . . . well, since his dad left. A boy needs a man he can look up to, and Jim—"

"How dare you suggest that I am incapable of raising my own son!" Red-faced, Naomi got to her feet. "He's my son, not your husband's and not yours. I make sure he has everything he needs, and I can assure you he would tell me if he wasn't happy being in the play. Sure, he's a twelve-year-old boy. He likes to be cool in front of his friends, so he acts like anything to do with school or Mom is a pain, but that doesn't mean he isn't really having fun. He loves acting. He's having a great time playing Peter Pan, and I'm sure—"

"No, Mom, I'm not."

They both turned to see Kenny standing in the doorway in a rumpled T-shirt and sweatpants with his left foot in a walking cast. His sandy hair stuck up all over and his eyes were bleary. Clearly their argument had awakened him.

"Kenny."

"I don't want to do it anymore, Mom, okay? I never wanted to in the first place. I guess . . . " He ducked his head, fingers twisting in the bottom of his shirt. "I should have told you, but I didn't want you to be mad. I should have told you, and then Luke's dad wouldn't be in trouble."

Naomi glared at Sofia. Softening, she turned back to her son. "Don't you worry about that, honey. That's for me to take care of. It's not your fault."

He shook his head, blue eyes filling with tears. "You don't understand, Mom. It *is* my fault. It wasn't an accident. Mr. Parker didn't leave the toolbox there by mistake. It was me."

Sofia caught her breath, understanding it all now.

"You mean you left the toolbox there, honey? And then it fell on you?"

Once more, Kenny shook his head. "No, Mom. I mean I *let* it fall on me. I *made* it fall on me." His lower lip trembled. "So I didn't have to be in the play anymore."

"Kenny." Naomi's eyes filled with tears and horrified realization. "Kenny, no."

"It was the tape measure, wasn't it, Kenny?" Sofia asked.

He winced and then reluctantly nodded. "I put the end of it under the toolbox. When I was in the right place, I pulled on it. After the toolbox fell on me, I reeled in the tape measure and threw it under the bench. But I didn't think anybody would get in trouble. Mr. Parker's been really nice to me. I didn't want him to get blamed."

Sofia nodded. "I thought that must have been what happened. It was the only thing that made sense."

Kenny bit his lip. "I . . . I did all the other things too. I'm sorry, Mrs. Parker, for ruining your backdrop and the costume and stuff. I thought if everything was messed up, they'd have to cancel the play." He wiped his nose with the back of his hand. "I don't want Mr. Parker to get in trouble because of me. Please, Mom, it was all my fault."

"Kenny," Naomi breathed again. "Why didn't you tell me?"

He looked at the floor and then pleadingly at his mother. "I didn't want you to be mad at me."

"Oh, baby." She went to him and wrapped him in her arms. "I'm so, *so* sorry. I never wanted you to think you couldn't tell me how you really felt." She hugged him even tighter, pressing her lips to his hair. Then she turned his face up to her. "Do you think Davy would like playing Peter Pan?"

He nodded, searching her face, looking relieved to see only gentle understanding there.

"And maybe," she added with a glance at Sofia, "Mr. Parker could still use some help finishing up the sets."

He nodded again, looking hopefully at Sofia.

"I'm sure he'd be happy to have you, Kenny. When you're feeling up to it. He says he's pretty amazed at how fast you've been learning things."

He shrugged a little, but there was shy pleasure in his eyes.

"All right," Naomi said, "we'll talk about all this more tomorrow. You'd better get back to bed now, and this time, stay there."

Kenny nodded. "Good night, Mrs. Parker."

Sofia smiled. "Good night, Kenny. Sweet dreams."

As soon as he was gone, Naomi sank down on the sofa, looking as if she didn't know what to say.

"Maybe I ought to go now," Sofia said, getting up. "I have to get started early in the morning."

Naomi nodded, still looking half-dazed. "How? How could I not have known?"

Sofia wanted to give her a hug, knowing how easy it was for even the most well-meaning mom to miss what her kids were really trying to tell her, but she didn't quite dare do that yet. Instead, she put a hand on Naomi's shoulder. "You know now. That's what's important."

Naomi dropped her head into her hands. "What he must think of me. My own son."

Sofia smiled, kneeling down so she could look into her face. "I think he understands more than you give him credit for."

Naomi looked as if she desperately wanted to believe her but didn't dare. "What makes you think that?"

"I could see it on his face and in the way he was trying so hard to make you happy."

Naomi shook her head. Whether it was out of remorse or disbelief, Sofia wasn't sure.

"Just ask him about it. I'll see you tomorrow."

With a little wave, Sofia went to the door.

"Sofia?"

Sofia stopped and looked back at her.

"I'll call that attorney first thing tomorrow and drop the lawsuit." She looked down. "I'm really sorry. I didn't notice how I was acting. I was so caught up in everything, I thought . . . I only wanted to do a good job and make sure the play was a success. I didn't realize everyone hated me."

Sofia went back to the sofa and sat down next to Naomi, and this time she did put her arm around her. "Everyone doesn't hate you. But, you know, they're just kids, not professional actors. It doesn't have to be perfect." Sofia let her mouth turn up at one corner. "And I bet if you let them have a little fun, it'll be a better play anyway."

Naomi nodded rapidly, not saying anything.

Sofia stood up again. "It'll be fine. Really it will."

Again Naomi nodded. "Kenny's foot is broken, but the doctor says there aren't any complications. He should be fine in a few weeks."

"That's wonderful news."

"I'll see you at dress rehearsal tomorrow." Naomi drew a

deep, steadying breath. "I'll call Davy before then and tell him he's the new Peter Pan."

Sofia smiled. "He'll be thrilled."

22

Bath, England
November 1799

"*H*ave you heard? Bonaparte has made himself First Consul of France."

From her knees, Cerise looked up at the countess, the pins in her mouth making her unable to do anything but nod.

"Thank goodness," said the woman, a smile on her pleasant English face. "The Terror is ended at last."

Cerise placed the last of the pins and smiled too. "Yes, my lady, thank God."

"But at least you and Monsieur Valérian made it away in time. I think you have prospered here on our little island."

Cerise looked fondly at her children playing on the floor of the workroom. They all had their father's dark eyes, but only the boy's hair was dark. The older girl's was moonlight pale and hung in shimmering waves down her back. And the youngest, curled up asleep near the hearth, had hardly any hair at all.

"How old are they now, madame?"

"Alexandre is four and Émilie will be seven next month. Our little Marie is nearly two."

"Ah," said the countess. "They make a pretty picture, madame, but then how could they not?"

Cerise bowed her head. "My lady is too kind. They are safe and well and happy. For that we thank le bon Dieu. We thank God."

She helped the countess out of her new gown and back into her old one. They exchanged the usual pleasantries, and then the countess hurried away.

Alexis came to Cerise's side, slipping one arm around her. "You deal with them well, mon ange. Always you do."

"I suppose it is easy to serve mere nobility when one has been attendant to a queen."

He laughed softly. "Do you miss those days, chérie, when we lived in a palace and every day were surrounded by royalty? And when you were of the nobility and not merely named so?"

She put her hand over the one at her waist, held it more tightly against her, and pressed herself closer to him as she did. "When I was always afraid, wondering if my clothes and my hair and every word were flawless? Wondering if I had angered such a one or some other and fearing someone else might be favored over me? Seeing the queen and knowing, for all her power, she was yet unhappy?" Still encircled by his arm, she turned to face him. "Wondering to whom I might be given in marriage, and having no say?"

"And so we find ourselves in England, with little to show for those days of extravagance and nothing to remind us of France."

"Nothing?" Cerise asked, her eyes falling on the silk fabric embroidered with golden fleurs-de-lis. "I have this remnant left from little Marie's namesake. I will treasure the memories of my time at Versailles always. Perhaps Marie will pass this along to her own daughter some day."

Alexis smiled down at Cerise, his velvet eyes warm. "But you might have had a noble husband and not merely a trumpery aristocrat."

She caressed his cheek and then slid her hand to the back of his neck, lifting her lips to his. "I have the noblest husband in all Christendom."

Cabot Falls, Vermont
Present Day

The audience burst into applause as the curtains closed and then opened again to reveal the entire cast. The applause grew louder as they took their bows.

When the lights went up, Sofia quickly squeezed past Gina, Rosa, and their families. "Meet you all back at the house?" she asked.

"Where else would we go? Nearly all of my good shoes are in your closet," Rosa replied with a wink. "Tell the guys they did a great job. Bravo! And we must celebrate a performance well done!"

Sofia smiled at her sister's theatrics and hurried backstage to see Jim and Luke. They were packing up the harnesses and everything else that made Peter Pan and the Darlings fly.

"Good job, guys!" She ruffled Luke's hair. "You didn't even drop anybody."

He laughed. "Mom!"

"Get your stuff now," she said, and then she looked at Jim. "We'll take the rest of this down tomorrow, right?"

He nodded. "Just don't want to leave anything too tempting out here, even for only one night."

"Good idea. But now it's all over, I'm ready to go home. Can you hurry?"

Jim saluted. "Aye-aye, Cap'n. Look lively there, sailor."

Luke giggled and quickened his pace. "Yes sir!"

"Mrs. Parker?" Davy scurried up the stage steps and behind the scenery. "What did you think? Did you like it?"

"I thought it was great."

She gave Davy a big hug, and he beamed at her from under his green hat with the little red feather.

"Did I do good?"

"You were great! Really great! I know your mom and dad are very proud of you."

He shrugged a little, grinning. "They're over there with Mrs. Moore. I guess she thinks I did okay too."

Naomi's eyes were shining, and she looked happier and more relaxed than Sofia had ever seen her.

"Yeah," Sofia said. "I'm sure she does." She searched the boy's face for a moment, and then she leaned down to him. "Davy, I know you and Jason and Connor didn't have anything to do with all the mischief that's been going on around here since the play started, but you three have been up to something. You want to tell me what it is?"

Davy bit his lip, glancing over at his parents. "It's . . . it's really nothing, Mrs. Parker. We didn't do anything wrong."

She gave him her best "I'm not buying it" look that usually worked on her own kids. "But what *did* you do?"

"Well, I couldn't let them starve."

She lifted one eyebrow. "Let who starve?"

He glanced at his parents once more and then beckoned for her to follow him. They went out the back door and toward some old packing crates.

"Where are we going?" she asked, wrapping her arms around herself against the chill of the night.

"Just here."

He shifted one of the boxes a little to one side, and she heard something move. He grinned at her, motioning for her to lean down. Tucked away in a blanket, their eyes shining in the streetlight, were three tabby kittens. They weren't very young; they had probably been born the previous spring.

"Somebody dumped them here," Davy said. "Connor and Jason and I heard them crying, but we knew our parents wouldn't let us keep them. So we made them a place to stay, and we've been bringing them food and water."

She smiled. "That was very sweet of you, Davy, but you know the school won't let you keep them out here. What if Mr. Trumbull found out?"

He gave her a mischievous little grin. "He found out the second day we were feeding them. He's been helping us." His grin faded. "It's not right for people to just dump animals out like that. They don't even know how to hunt or anything."

"No, it's not right." She put her arm around him. "Come on, let's go back in where it's warm. Did you ask your parents about keeping them? Or maybe just one of them?"

He shook his head. "I don't think they'd let me."

"Well, why don't you ask them? Whatever they say, we should probably make sure the kittens are taken care of. At least in a shelter, don't you think?"

He bit his lip, eyes pleading. "They'll kill them, won't they?"

"Not the one I'm thinking of. They'll take care of them until they can find them good homes"—she hustled him inside—"where it's warm."

He rubbed his bare arms, looking toward his parents again. "Do you think they might? I mean, for Christmas?"

"Go ask them!" Smiling, she gave him a little push forward, and he sprinted away.

"Where'd you go?" Jim asked, putting one arm around her and then shivering. "You're freezing."

She chuckled and snuggled against him. "I found out what our little Peter Pan and his Lost Boys have been up to along with our stonehearted janitor."

He lifted one eyebrow. "Oh?"

"They've been taking care of some kittens out back. Can you believe it?"

Jim looked incredulous and then started to laugh. "That old coot? I would never have thought it of him."

"Neither would I." She shook her head. "I guess you never know—"

"Sofia?"

Sofia and Jim both turned to see Naomi and Kenny behind them.

"I just wanted to thank you again," Naomi said. "You've both been a great help." She glanced at her son. "With everything."

Before they could reply, she waved and hurried Kenny away.

Sofia shook her head. "As I was saying, I guess you never know when someone who looks hard-boiled might turn out to be a cream puff deep inside."

"Or," Jim said, "when some little mouse might stand up and surprise you."

She nodded, taking his hand and tugging him toward the door. Yes, Kenny had surprised her, and so had Cerise. And maybe, now and then, Sofia had surprised herself—especially with her baking skills. Her recent catering job had been so successful that she'd been hired by an attendee to cater a high-profile wedding.

Jim opened the door so she could step into the cold December air and through the snow that reflected the Christmastime stars. Watching them leave, Mr. Trumbull gave them his usual scowl, and Sofia, feeling it, turned just in time to see an unexpected wink. She smiled in return.

The old softy.

Learn more about Annie's fiction books at

AnniesFiction.com

We've designed the Annie's Fiction website especially for you!

Access your e-books • Read sample chapters • Manage your account

Choose from one of these great series:

Amish Inn Mysteries	Chocolate Shoppe Mysteries
Annie's Attic Mysteries	Creative Woman Mysteries
Annie's Mysteries Unraveled	Hearts of Amish Country
Annie's Quilted Mysteries	Secrets of the Castleton Manor Library
Annie's Secrets of the Quilt	Victorian Mansion Flower Shop Mysteries
Antique Shop Mysteries	

What are you waiting for? Visit us now at **AnniesFiction.com!**